I dashed t[illegible] tening,
and pushed it open. Frigid air flowed
in to wrap me in its cold embrace.

A bright moon floated in the sky overhead. By its light, I could see that Kai's window was wide open. The street below me sparkled with hoarfrost. In the rime, I could see a single set of footprints leaving Kai's building and heading down the street.

I don't remember putting on my stockings and shoes. Don't remember throwing my winter cloak around my shoulders. What I remember clearly is standing in the street, gazing down that straight line of footsteps. It led to the corner, then turned, vanishing from sight.

Gone. My heart thundered in my chest. *Gone. Gone. Gone.*

It did no good for my mind to assert that Kai was safe in bed, for it to reason with me that the footprints could belong to anyone. My heart knew the truth.

Kai was gone. He had followed the Winter

"Once upon a Time" is timeless with these retold tales:

Beauty Sleep
Cameron Dokey

Midnight Pearls
Debbie Viguié

Snow
Tracy Lynn

Water Song
Suzanne Weyn

The Storyteller's Daughter
Cameron Dokey

Before Midnight
Cameron Dokey

Golden
Cameron Dokey

The Rose Bride
Nancy Holder

Sunlight and Shadow
Cameron Dokey

The Crimson Thread
Suzanne Weyn

Belle
Cameron Dokey

The Night Dance
Suzanne Weyn

Wild Orchid
Cameron Dokey

The Diamond Secret
Suzanne Weyn

Winter's Child

Cameron Dokey

SIMON PULSE
New York London Toronto Sydney

This book is a work of fiction. Any references to historical events, real people, or real locales are used fictitiously. Other names, characters, places, and incidents are the product of the author's imagination, and any resemblance to actual events or locales or persons, living or dead, is entirely coincidental.

SIMON PULSE
An imprint of Simon & Schuster Children's Publishing Division
1230 Avenue of the Americas, New York, NY 10020
First Simon Pulse paperback edition September 2009

For information about special discounts for bulk purchases, please contact
Simon & Schuster Special Sales at 1-866-506-1949 or
business@simonandschuster.com.
The Simon & Schuster Speakers Bureau can bring authors to your
live event. For more information or to book an event contact the
Simon & Schuster Speakers Bureau at 1-866-248-3049 or visit
our website at www.simonspeakers.com.
The text of this book was set in Adobe Jenson.
Manufactured in the United States of America
2 4 6 8 10 9 7 5 3
Library of Congress Control Number 2009924828
ISBN 978-1-4169-7560-1
ISBN 978-1-4169-8532-7 (eBook)

To Annette Pollert, editor extraordinaire, with many thanks

Prologue

A Few Words Concerning Stories

The world is full of countless stories, all being told at the same time.

Some are so quiet you have to strain your ears to hear them. Stories like the one the grocer tells to the first autumn apples as they jostle for position on his shelves. He murmurs as he polishes them with his flannel sleeve, promising to make them shine so brightly that every single apple will take a journey in a market basket to be made into a pie before the sun goes down.

Only a little louder is the tale that the sea captain's young daughter tells her rag doll in the dark of night. She huddles in her bed, listening to the wind moan. "*Soon,*" she whispers into one rag-doll ear. "*Soon Papa will return, safe and whole.*" That is what the wind is saying, she promises the doll. *Papa will come home again. He will not leave us.* Outside, the wind continues its endless sob and moan. But as long as her lips have the power to tell the tale, the sea captain's daughter's eyes stay dry.

Then there are the tales that shout; stories that can shake the rooftops with their wonder: the tales that sweethearts tell. Most wonderful of these are the ones when both the tales and the love prove true.

And then there are the everyday tales, the tales that make the world go around. Stories children tell themselves so they believe they're growing up faster than is possible; tales parents tell each other as they cling together, watching their youngsters strike out on their own; tales the old folks tell to help them remember what it felt like to be young; stories the voices of the living chant over the graves of the dead, mourning those whose storytelling days are done.

Pick any time of the day or night and somewhere, everywhere, stories are being told. They overlap and flow across one another, then pull away again just as waves do upon a shore. It is this knack that stories have of rubbing up against one another that makes the world an interesting place, a place of greater possibility than it would be if we told our tales alone.

This is impossible, of course. Make no mistake, everyone's story touches someone else's. And every brush of one life tale upon another, be it ever so gentle, creates something new: a pathway that wasn't there before. The possibility to create a new tale.

In this story—which, as I'm sure you've already figured out, is not one but several all flowing together, parting ways only to bump into one another again—in this story, something very remarkable takes place:

All paths begin and end at the door of the Winter Child.

One

Story the First

In Which the Winter Child Receives Her Name, and All the Tales That Make Up This Story Are Thereby Set in Motion

Many years ago, when the world was much younger than it is today, a king and queen dwelt together in a castle made of ice and snow. No doubt this may seem uncomfortable to you, but as this royal couple ruled over a kingdom where there was so much ice and snow that not a single day went by without some sight of both, the king and queen had become accustomed to their situation. It suited them just fine. They found nothing unusual about their circumstance, in fact.

But I am straying from my path already, and I've no more than packed my bag and started out the door.

The king and queen had been married for several years when the stories you are about to read were preparing to begin. The royal couple had loved each other truly when first they had wed, but, as the years went by, the queen began to fear the march of time. She began to ask herself a series of impossible questions, questions with no answers:

If her looks should start to fade, as inevitably they must, would the king still care for her? Or did he love her for her appearance alone?

In all fairness, it must be acknowledged that the queen was very lovely. Her face was a perfect oval. Her lips were the color of the bright red berries that flourished even in the depths of winter, and her skin was as white as snow. Her eyes gleamed like two jet buttons, and her hair was a waterfall of black as dark as a night without stars.

In equal fairness, it must be acknowledged that, by giving in to her fear, the queen performed a great disservice, both to herself and to her husband. The king had not fallen in love with her simply because of the loveliness of her face, but also for the strength and beauty of her heart.

But giving in to her fear was precisely what the queen did. Her heart didn't even put up a fight. The moment that happened, all was lost, though the queen didn't realize this at the time. As soon as fear's occupation of the queen's heart was complete, she retreated to the castle's highest tower. All she took for company were her baby daughter, just six months old, and a mirror made of polished ice.

First days, and then weeks, went by. The queen sat in a hard-backed chair, gazing at her face for hour after hour, searching for the first sign that her beauty—and the king's love—were poised to take flight. The king visited the tower morning, noon, and night. The nursemaids came and went, caring for the princess. The housemaids came and went, dusting the room and lighting the fires. The king sent first the royal physician, and then every other healer in the land to see if any could cure the queen's strange malady.

None of it made any difference. Nothing the king did or said could penetrate the fear that had captured the queen's heart. And so, as the weeks threatened to slide on into months and still the queen's heart refused to listen, something terrible began to transpire. The king's love began to falter, for not even the strongest love can survive all on its own. Love cannot thrive simply by being offered. Sooner or later it must be accepted and reciprocated. It must be seen for what it is and nourished according to its needs, or it will die.

The queen's face remained as beautiful as ever. But the king's love could not stay the course charted by his wife's fearful heart. His love began to diminish with every minute of every day that the queen stayed in the tower, until at last the morning dawned when the king awoke and discovered that his love for the queen was altogether gone. And in this way, the queen's own actions brought about the result she had so feared: The king no longer loved her.

Love must go somewhere, however, and the king still had one family member left, his baby daughter. Determined that she should not suffer because her mother had eyes only for herself, the king decided to love the princess twice as much as he had before.

The baby had her mother's coloring. She, too, had hair and eyes as black as night. Her skin was as pale as fine white linen, and her mouth, a perfect little red rosebud. This caused the king both pain and joy. Every time he gazed into his daughter's face, as he did each morning, noon, and night, it seemed to him that he felt the clutch of fear wrap itself around his love.

Search though he might, the king could find nothing of himself in his daughter's face. In every particular, she seemed to be her mother's child. The queen's fate was hardly turning out as might have been predicted, let alone desired. The princess's resemblance to her mother could not help but make the king wonder about his daughter's own fate. What might it hold in store?

Now, it was the custom in the land of ice and snow for mothers to bestow names upon their newborns. Every family followed this tradition, from the royal couple to the woodcutter and his wife. Most people named their children right away, for it was dangerous to let a child go without a name for too long. Without a name, it is hard to develop a sense of direction. Without a name, it is difficult to set out on your life's journey and so discover who you are.

This is not to say that any name will do, of course. In fact, it's just the opposite. Every child must be given her or his true and proper name, and this is a task that cannot be rushed. It takes time.

So when at first days, and then weeks, went by and still the baby princess had no name, though it made the king uneasy, he kept it to himself. But as the weeks slid into months that added up to half a year, the king's uneasiness turned into genuine alarm. Day after day, the infant princess lay in a basket by the tower window, kicking off her blankets no matter how tightly her nursemaids wrapped her up. This, the nursemaids took to be a sign.

"She is trying to escape her destiny," whispered the first, as the nursemaids sat together near the kitchen fire one night. They were having a bedtime snack of tea and scones.

"Oh, don't be daft," the second replied. She took a gulp of tea, then winced as it burned her tongue. "There's not a soul alive can do a thing like that."

But it was the third nursemaid who came closest to the mark. She sipped her tea, for she was more cautious.

"She's only six months old," the third nursemaid remarked. "The princess doesn't have the faintest idea what her destiny is yet. And she won't, poor mite. Not until she has a name to call her own."

Not long after this conversation took place, there came an afternoon when, just like always, the queen sat in her hard-backed chair gazing at her reflection. Her baby daughter lay, kicking her legs, in a basket on a nearby window seat. The window was open for, though cold, the sun was shining and the day was fine. High above the castle, so high as to render the legs of the baby princess so small they were almost invisible, the North Wind was passing by.

Now, the North Wind is a cross wind, a contrary and unpredictable blusterer. The plain and simple truth of the matter is that the North Wind hates to be cold. But as bringing cold is the North Wind's reason for existence, it really has no choice. This is why, in the dead of winter, the North Wind howls so. It's lamenting its own fate and wailing a warning. It will do some mischief if it can, and never mind the consequences.

And that's precisely what happened that day at the palace. The North Wind passed by with mischief on its mind.

It did not care that the sun was shining and the day was fine. It could not bring about such things itself, and so they provoked only jealousy in the North Wind's soul. So when it spied an infant lying unwatched and unprotected by an open window, the North Wind swooped down to take a closer look. Perhaps it might be able to use the baby to conjure up enough mischief to summon clouds that would blot out the sun.

But no sooner did the North Wind come in through the window than it caught sight of the queen gazing at her reflection in the mirror made of ice. The North Wind was so struck by the queen's beauty that it forgot completely why it had come. If it had been possible for something to deprive the North Wind of breath, the queen's beauty would have done so.

But no matter how the North Wind tried to get the queen's attention, frisking around the hem of her skirts, teasing the ends of her midnight-dark hair, nothing compelled the queen to look up. She never even shivered, as if she didn't feel the North Wind's presence at all. Instead, the queen's eyes stayed fixed upon her mirror and her reflection. Thoroughly vexed, for it was not accustomed to being ignored, the North Wind swirled around the tower room. There, on the window seat, was the infant who had drawn it down to the castle in the first place.

Aha! the North Wind thought. It dashed to the window and caught the child up in its arms, sending the basket and cushions beneath her out the open window in a great *whoosh* of air. Surely whisking away the beautiful woman's infant would get her attention.

Sadly for all concerned, it did not.

The North Wind carried the princess straight out the window, and still the queen did not so much as stir or turn around. When it realized this, the North Wind behaved true to form. Having stirred up some mischief, the North Wind lost interest and released the child, letting her fall.

Down, down, down the baby princess plummeted, kicking her legs the entire time. She fell past the window where her mother's ladies in waiting sat busy with the castle mending. Past the window where her father's pages were dusting the leather spines of all the books on the library shelves. And finally, past the royal study where her father sat at an open window of his own, jotting down notes for a State of the Kingdom address he would be making in about a week's time.

At the sight of his daughter hurtling inexorably downward, the king gave a great cry. He abandoned his papers, leaped to his feet, and dashed down the stairs from his study to the castle's front door. He hadn't a chance of reaching his daughter before the ground did. The situation was simple as that and, even as the king ran for all he was worth, he knew this in his heart. But just as the king was sure his heart would burst with fear and love combined, the unseen forces that shape the world around us interfered for a second time.

Just before the princess hit the ground, a different wind caught the baby in its arms. It was a small and playful wind, a delicate wind, a harbinger of the spring that comes after the North Wind passes by. A wind like this was not about to watch a baby be dashed to pieces, particularly not on such a beautiful day.

With a touch as gentle as a shower of flower petals, the wind set the princess on a nearby snowbank. And this was where the king found her moments later, no longer kicking her legs, for the Spring Wind had carried away the princess's blanket, but had left her otherwise completely unharmed.

"Unharmed." It's a nice word, isn't it? A comforting word, though not quite all-encompassing. "Unharmed" is not the same as "unchanged," after all. And "changed" is precisely what the princess was.

The baby's hair, once as dark as the feathers of a raven, was now as white as the snowbank on which she rested. Her eyes, no longer dark, had become the fine and delicate blue of a winter sky. Her skin always had been white, but now it seemed so thin that the king could see the blue veins weaving their intricate patterns, like lace, beneath the surface. The princess's lips, previously as red as a rosebud, had faded to the pale pink of that same rose now kissed by a winter's frost.

The embrace of the North Wind had changed the princess forever. She had become a Winter Child.

The king loved her no less for this, however. In fact, as he cradled his daughter against his thundering heart, the king might even have loved her more. For now, at least a portion of her destiny seemed clear:

She must walk the ways of a Winter Child.

A Winter Child does not tread the same paths as the rest of us. The touch of the North Wind lingers on a Winter Child long after the wind itself is gone. There is only one way to remove this touch, and so return a Winter Child to her true and original form. She must help to right some great and terrible wrong. She must atone for a sadness that was not of her making.

This is what it means to be a Winter Child.

No sooner did the king come to realize all this than he realized he was angry. Angry with the queen, his wife, a mother so intent upon herself that she had failed to see the danger to her daughter, let alone to save her from it.

And so, still cradling the baby in his arms, the king returned to the castle and climbed all the way to the topmost tower, taking the steps two at a time.

He burst into the chamber where the queen still sat, gazing at herself. She had not even noticed that the baby was gone.

"Look what our daughter has become! Look what you have helped to make her!" the king cried.

The king held out the baby toward the queen, and finally, the queen looked up from the mirror made of ice. The coldness of the North Wind had utterly failed to catch her attention, but the heat in her husband's voice turned the queen's head as if pulled by a cord. Even accustomed as she was to gazing at nothing but her own features, the queen could see at once that something was terribly wrong.

"But I never—," the queen began.

"Yes, I know you never," the king cried passionately, cutting her off. "You never even noticed our daughter was missing, because you never see anyone but yourself!"

He advanced into the room, still holding the infant out in front of him, and now the queen could clearly see the changes in her daughter for herself. She felt a fine trembling begin in the pit of her stomach and spread to her limbs. For the first time since coming to the land of ice and snow, the queen felt cold. Cold with the apprehension that something dreadful was about to happen, something that now could not be turned aside.

"How I curse the mirror that you clasp so tightly!" the king went on. "More tightly than you have ever clasped our child. How I wish your mirror could show you the coldness of your heart. I wish that it could show what lies beneath your beauty. I wish it could expose your flaws."

Here, I will give you some important information, so important you may even wish to write it down and keep it somewhere safe. Put it in a place where you can take it out and look at it from time to time. And that important information is this: It is very dangerous to utter a wish and a curse at the same time.

That's ridiculous, you may answer. *Surely the two would cancel each other out.*

Don't you believe it. Not for a moment. Instead of canceling each other out, each magnifies the other, giving it more power, until both the wish and the curse have enough power to come true.

That is precisely what happened in the tower room that day. No sooner had the king finished speaking than the queen uttered a piercing cry. She flung the mirror away with all her strength. It struck the wall, shattering into pieces too numerous to count. Most flew out the window and were borne away by the wind. Only one did not. This icy fragment struck the baby princess and embedded itself deep in her heart.

The power of a wish and a curse together now had done its work. Each had fed upon the other's energy, growing in strength, until both were granted at the same time. In that instant, the queen's mirror had revealed not just her outer beauty, but also her innermost flaw. What she had seen so pained and horrified her that the queen's heart shattered into pieces too numerous to count, just as the mirror had. She perished on the spot. All that remained of her beauty was her daughter's pale and serious face.

Her daughter, the Winter Child, who now had a shard of cursed and icy mirror embedded in her heart.

The king sank to his knees, still cradling his baby girl in his arms. What his own heart felt in that moment, no living soul will ever know. But now, with cold tears streaming down his cheeks, the king spoke one thing more. He spoke his daughter's name aloud.

Deirdre. That was what he called her. *Sorrow* was the name the king gave to his only child. Then he bowed his head and, at last, his tears grew warm.

For now the king wept not just for what would be, but for all the things that could be no more. He wept for the fate of his wife, whom he had once loved so deeply, and for that of his young daughter, now forever altered by the North Wind's touch. As the king rocked her in his arms, dampening her pale face with his tears, he vowed that he would spend the rest of his life trying to prepare his daughter for whatever lay in store for her as a Winter Child.

But as to what, precisely, that might be . . . for that we must move on to another story.

Two

Story the Second

In Which Grace Takes Up the Tale and Introduces Us to Kai

I cannot imagine a world without Kai.

Part of this is simple mathematics. I've never known a world without him in it, for he was born three days before me. Part of it is simply love. Except that love is rarely simple, even when you think it is. Or maybe I should say that love is rarely simple in the *way* you think it is. I'm living proof of that.

Kai and I grew up together, side by side. We lived at the very tops of two old neighboring buildings that leaned toward each other ever so slightly, like sweethearts who couldn't bear the thought of being kept apart. The rooftops were so close together we could place a single plank across the gap between them and walk from one rooftop to the other. We did this every summer after Kai was strong enough to put the board in place and our courage was strong enough to carry us across.

Kai never looked down.

I always did. This was a difference between us, right from the start, a difference that became more pronounced as time went on. Kai's eyes sought out nearby things, while my eyes much preferred to search for far-off ones.

"Grace, don't," Kai used to plead when I would stop partway between my rooftop and his to wave at Herre Johannes, the flower merchant, as he pulled his horse and cart up in front of our buildings' front doors, far below. "Don't look down. It's dangerous. You'll fall."

"Of course I won't fall, silly," I answered back. I lifted one foot to take a step, then held it poised in midair. This worried Kai most of all.

"You can't fall if your feet know where they're supposed to be." And with this, I always put my foot back down on the board and continued on my way.

"Yes, but what if the board has a change of heart about letting you walk on it in the first place?" Kai would query every time he grasped my hand and pulled me to the safety of his rooftop.

This was our standard discussion, not quite serious enough to be called a true argument. I always insisted that I would be all right in the end if only I knew where to place my feet. Usually, it was as simple and straightforward as putting one in front of the other. Kai was equally insistent that even the most straightforward of paths could turn out to be more complicated than it seemed at first. Which meant, in turn, of course, that even the most carefully placed footsteps could be sent awry entirely without warning.

Perhaps it will come as a surprise, then, when I tell you that most of the time it was Kai who made the trip from his rooftop to mine. This, despite the fact that he disliked heights. In addition to saving me from potential foolishness and danger, the plain and simple truth was that our rooftop was much more pleasant.

My grandmother, my oma, had one of the best green thumbs in town. Our rooftop caught the rain just like everybody else's did, but my oma knew just what to do with the rain that fell on ours. Almost every square inch of our roof was filled with a pot or planter of some kind. Some held fruit and vegetables that we would eat fresh in summer, then preserve to eat during the long winter months. But most of the pots were filled with flowers.

There were geraniums red as firebrands and marigolds as bright as spun gold. In early spring, sweet peas fluttered like flocks of tiny purple finches. In the autumn, mums clustered together like schoolchildren in their new winter coats, preparing for the cold.

The flowers did more than bring us pleasure. They also brought in much-needed income. This money was important, for it was just my oma and me at home. My father, Oma's son, had been a soldier stationed in a faraway land. He died in a skirmish when I was very young. My mother had loved my father so much that, rather than stay at home in safety after I was born, she had left me behind in Oma's care and followed her husband and the drum.

When word of my father's death was brought to my mother, she left the camp and walked to the edge of the river along whose banks the battle had been fought. There, she filled the pockets of her apron with stones. Then she waded out until the swift current swept her feet from under her and the stones in her pockets pulled her down to the river's floor. In this way, I lost both my parents on the very same day.

No doubt you're waiting for me to say that I missed them, but it would be more truthful to say that I missed the *idea* of them most of all. They had departed, first our city and then this world, when I was so small as to have had no true memory of either of them. I had only Oma's memories and her stories of my father as a little boy. Much as I treasured these tales, they were not quite the same as memories I might have created had I known my parents myself.

I took careful note of the other children's parents as I grew up, however. Children are always interested in what other children have that they do not. It seemed to me that some of the parents I saw were happy together, but many were not. Happiness can be difficult to hold onto, I think, when your body is weary, your stomach is never quite full, and your hands are cold even in the summertime.

Take Kai's parents, for instance. His father worked in the coal mines just outside of town. In the summer, whistles blasted, summoning the miners to work just as the sun came up, but in winter, they did so long before the sun even had its eye on the horizon. Kai's father walked to work in the dark, and he labored in the dark. In the dark, he walked home. Then he had many flights of stairs to climb before he could take off his boots outside his own front door. To keep the choking dust of his labors out of the house as much as possible, Kai's mother cleaned out her husband's boots in the hall.

On many nights, or so Kai once told me, his father never said a word. He was so weary, it was as if the coal dust had closed up his throat. But sometimes, raised voices lifted themselves into the air and flew from Kai's building to mine. On those nights, I could hear them, even when it was winter and the windows were tightly closed.

After those nights, I would awaken to find Kai asleep at the foot of my bed. He would be curled up in the nest of blankets Oma kept for him in the trunk that had once held her trousseau. Kai's mother would come for him in the morning, her face pale, her mouth pinched so tightly it was a wonder she could drink Oma's sweet, dark tea. Circles would be inked beneath her eyes.

Kai and I never spoke about those mornings, just as we never spoke about the nights that preceded them. But when his father died, killed by the very earth itself when a section of the mine collapsed, Kai wept. His mother sobbed so long and hard that she had to be carried home from the burial ground. That was the first time I realized love was not as simple as you might suppose. To me, Kai's father had seemed a cold, hard man, a man designed to frighten. But why would you weep over the loss of someone you feared?

This was also the first time I wondered whether or not Kai's eyes, so good at seeing what was near, could see things invisible to mine.

Both before and after Kai's father's death, his mother took in sewing. Oma and I had done this as well, starting when I was old enough to use a needle without poking myself. During the winter months the three of us often worked together. We took turns: one week in front of the stove at our house and the next week in front of the one at Kai's. That way, we weren't heating two houses at once.

I hate to sew.

I think it's one of the reasons my feet itch to take to the road and my eyes want nothing better than to be fixed on the horizon line. Sewing requires you to sit still, to look only at what is close to you. Even if you're setting a sleeve into an armhole, so that you are stitching around in a circle, sewing is all about that which is straight. Straight stitches, straight seams, straight lines. Kai sewed with us until he became old enough to be apprenticed to Herre Lindstrom, the watchmaker. He was always much better at it than I was.

The one good thing about sewing, however, was that my grandmother and Kai's mother would tell stories to help pass the time. Kai's mother had been born in the south. Her stories were often full of sunshine and warmth. But Oma had been raised in the far, far north. Her tales were comprised of ice and snow. It was she who first told us the tale of a girl forever altered by the North Wind, the tale of the Winter Child.

"Her name is Deirdre," my oma would say. "A word for sorrow, for sorrow and the fate of a Winter Child are intertwined."

"But why, Oma?" I would always ask, even after I had heard the story of Deirdre the Winter Child many, many times.

The fact that anybody, even a girl in a story, had a name like Sorrow always struck a strange chord in my heart. I liked my own name, Grace, just fine. But I don't think my affection for it made me swell-headed. I wasn't making any particular claim to being *graceful* because of it, and I certainly wasn't claiming to be better than anyone else. I can be impatient, and I have a nasty temper. I know these things well enough.

But my name did make me feel safe, somehow, as if it carved out a particular place for me in the world—even if I didn't quite know yet what that place would be. Being named Sorrow seemed a terrible fate.

"A Winter Child is unlike any other child on earth," my oma went on. "She has been touched by the North Wind, enfolded in its arms."

"All of us have felt the touch of the wind," Kai said. But he shivered, as if the memory of how the North Wind felt on a winter day was enough to make him cold.

"True," my oma replied. "But a Winter Child has felt more of the North Wind than either you or I have, Kai. We feel only the brush of its passing. It does not truly see us as it hurries by.

"But a Winter Child is chosen, swept up in the North Wind's arms. People are not made to be so close to the forces of nature. They have the power to alter us. Before a Winter Child can be as she was before, she must remove all traces of the North Wind's touch by righting some great wrong."

"That hardly seems fair," I remarked.

"Righting a great wrong is not a bad thing," Kai countered before my grandmother could reply. His eyes were fixed on his sewing, but his voice was stubborn. "I think it's brave and noble, not a cause for sorrow at all."

"Children," Kai's mother said chidingly, "let Frue Andersen tell the story."

"No, no," my oma said with a smile. "I don't mind the interruptions. It is true that righting a great wrong is not a bad thing in and of itself," my grandmother continued, and I battled back a spurt of irritation that she'd addressed Kai's objection rather than mine.

"Though doing so is often very hard. The path is easiest to walk when you choose it for yourself. But such a choice is not granted to a Winter Child."

I heard Kai pull in a breath, as if to speak again. I put my foot on top of his and pressed down, hard.

"What wrong must Deirdre set to right, Oma?" I inquired.

"The wrong committed by her parents," my grandmother replied. "You remember I told you how, when the queen's mirror shattered, all the pieces flew out the window and were carried away on the wind, all but the one that pierced her daughter's heart?"

I paused to carefully finish a seam before I answered. More than once I had been forced to take out stitches and do work over again after being caught up in one of Oma's stories.

"I remember," I said when the thread was knotted, the end snipped, and the seam done. I gave the sleeve a gentle tug, testing to see how my stitches held.

"Careful," Kai teased, as if he were seeking revenge for my stepping on his foot. "You'll pull it right back out again."

I stuck out my tongue.

"Those pieces flew throughout the world," my oma went on, "still filled with the magic of a wish and a curse combined. Each and every one found its way into a human heart. The persons so wounded have been changed forever in a terrible way: They are incapable of seeing with the eyes of true love."

There was a momentary silence while both Kai and I considered this.

"But . . . ," he said.

"How?" I asked at precisely the same time.

My oma smiled. "A heart that carries a sliver of that icy mirror is not what it was before," she explained. "It now contains both less and more. But the *more* that it contains is what creates the *less,* and so such a heart is at war with itself."

My oma paused, looking from me to Kai, and then back to me, as if waiting to see which one of us would figure out this riddle first.

"Fear," Kai suddenly burst out. "That's what the piece of mirror adds."

"Fear, indeed," my oma said. "You are right, Kai."

"But wait," I objected, doing my best not to show how irritated I was that Kai had figured it out first. "I thought the curse of the mirror was that it showed the queen her innermost flaw."

"You are right as well, Grace," my grandmother said. "Think about it for a moment. Why did the queen spend so much time at her mirror in the first place?"

"Because she was afraid," I answered slowly. "Afraid her beauty would fade and the king would stop loving her." I fell silent for a moment, considering what I could now see was the logical conclusion. "So fear was the queen's innermost flaw."

"I think it must have been, don't you?" my grandmother responded. "I've always thought that, when the queen looked in the mirror for that last time, she saw that she was just as beautiful as she had always been. Her face had not changed at all. Her beauty had not diminished, but still the king's love had fled.

"In that instant, the queen realized what she had done. She had brought the very woe she dreaded upon herself by giving in to her fear and closing off her heart. And her heart, grown smaller by staying so tightly wrapped, could not expand again. It could not contain this bitter knowledge and her fear all at once. Her heart shattered, just as she had shattered the mirror."

"And she perished in that same instant," I murmured, as I remembered what came next.

"She did." My grandmother nodded. "But she left behind her child and countless others, all with a sliver of ice in their hearts. So the wrong the Winter Child must right also was decided in the instant of her mother's death.

"To travel the world in search of all those wounded hearts and to mend them, one by one."

"But that could take forever," Kai protested.

"It will take as long as it must," my grandmother replied. "When the Winter Child turned sixteen," she went on, in a tone of voice that signaled she was returning to her storytelling and would tolerate no more interruptions, "the age when many young heroes begin their quests, the very day she turned sixteen, Deirdre, the Winter Child, set out on her journey.

"She put on a dress of linen, fine as gossamer. Over it she tied a woolen cloak as white as snow. She laced her feet into a pair of crystal boots as sturdy as the stars. She took a staff of pale ash wood into her hand, and she kissed her father the king good-bye. Then she turned and walked away from the palace made of ice, and she left the land of ice and snow behind.

"She did not look back, not even once. Though she must have wanted to, I think, don't you?"

I sat for a moment, my hands resting on the sewing in my lap, trying to imagine what it must be like to leave your home. Not because you wanted to, but because you must. Because you must right a wrong not your own.

Oh yes, I thought. *She must have wanted to look back very, very much.*

"She has been traveling the world ever since, seeking out and mending those damaged hearts, one by one. As long as Deirdre is on her journey, the magic of her quest embraces her, just as the arms of the North Wind did, so very long ago. She will never grow a day older, for she cannot continue her own life until her task is done. For most of us, the Winter Child is invisible, for she is not made to be seen by ordinary eyes.

"Even so," my oma continued in a hushed and reverent tone, "in the silence after a winter storm has ceased to howl, in the soft whisper of a morning snowfall, in the way the moonlight sparkles over new-fallen snow, you can feel when she has been nearby, ever searching. You can sense the presence of the Winter Child."

"But . . . ," Kai said yet again, and with that single word, he broke the storytelling spell.

"Oh, for goodness' sake," I cried. "Why must you always take everything apart to see how it works? Can't you just close your eyes and enjoy the story?"

"Grace," my grandmother said softly.

I immediately fell silent, for I knew that tone. All of us have heard some version of it at one time or another from those who love us most: the sound that says, *I am disappointed in you. That was badly done.*

"I'm sorry, Oma," I mumbled.

My grandmother fixed her dark eyes on me, but she said nothing. I gave an inward sigh. I love my oma with all my heart, but there's no denying her will of iron. She says I am like her in this, but I'm not so sure. For when my will comes up against hers, mine is always the one that bends.

"I'm sorry, Kai," I said, for my grandmother's point, of course, was that she was not the one who truly deserved my apology. "Please, go on."

"I just want to know one more thing," Kai said, and I could hear him struggling to keep the surliness out of his voice.

"And what is that?" my grandmother asked.

"What about the heart of the Winter Child? Who will mend that?"

At this, Kai's mother, Frue Holmgren, who had been silent for so long I'd almost forgotten that she was there, made a small sound. She performed a strange gesture, as if trying to snatch Kai's words right out of the air.

"Ah," my grandmother said with a sigh. "Now you have come to the heart of the Winter Child's tale, Kai.

"Even if Deirdre finds all the other wounded hearts and mends them, one by one, dissolving all the slivers of ice, driving out fear so that the hearts may know true love, there is still the matter of who will mend the Winter Child's own heart.

"Does the task fall to her or to someone else? No telling of the story I have ever heard has answered this question."

"Then perhaps," I said, determined not to let Kai outdo me when it came to observation, "the solution lies not in her tale at all, but in someone else's."

"Perhaps," agreed my oma.

There was a moment's silence. Kai stared down at his sewing. Out of the corner of my eye, I saw my oma reach out and take Frue Holmgren by the hand. And suddenly, I realized how late it was. The room was close and warm, and I was tired.

"I still think the king gave his daughter the wrong name," Kai said. "He should not have named her Sorrow."

Oma squeezed Frue Holmgren's fingers, and then let them go. "What name would you have chosen?" she inquired.

Kai looked up, his eyes fierce as they stared at my grandmother's face. "Hope," he said. "That's really what she brings, isn't it? So that's what her father should have named her."

My grandmother's expression softened. But as she leaned to place the palm of one hand against Kai's cheek, I was astonished to see that tears had risen in her eyes.

"Your true love will be fortunate in your heart, I think," she said. "For it is strong and whole. So will your love be, when you choose to give it."

With that, Oma leaned back and took up her sewing, and none of us said anything more.

Three

My grandmother told us many stories, but somehow, it was always the tale of the Winter Child that Kai and I loved best of all. Awakening in the morning, we imagined we saw the flare of her gossamer skirts in the patterns the ice formed outside our windows overnight. We heard the sound of her crystal boots in the noise the ice made as it scoured the walls and roof through the long, dark winter nights. Somehow, these flights of fancy helped to make our own winters more bearable.

Winter is not just a passing fancy in the land of my birth. It comes early and stays late. It can be beautiful, but it is also fierce and cunning, not to be ignored. Looking for traces of the Winter Child, wondering how many hearts she would mend that year, kept Kai and me busy until spring returned and we could be outdoors.

Even then, however, Kai always seemed to take the story more seriously than I did. It was as if, in his own heart, he didn't think of it as a made-up tale at all. Even as he used his sharp eyes to look closely at the world and so discover how it worked, Kai kept this one flight of fancy: He believed in the Winter Child.

As time went on, of course, we had less and less time for stories. We were both growing up. All too soon, our next birthdays would bring us to sixteen, the same age as the Winter Child herself. Kai had long since grown too old for staying at home. At twelve, he'd been apprenticed to Herre Lindstrom, who made and repaired clocks and watches.

Spending hour after hour hunched over all of those intricate pieces—springs so small and fine that if you dropped one it would disappear into the carpet and never be seen again, cogs with teeth and gaps between them designed to fit together in just one way and no other, even holding the tiny tools for such delicate work in my hands would have made me want to run screaming from the room. But Kai loved his hours in the watchmaker's shop.

"Everything makes sense, Grace," he said one afternoon, as we were walking together. Most days, when my sewing was done, I would leave home a little early to meet Kai, and we would walk home from Herre Lindstrom's shop. It was one of the few times when we were alone. There were not as many opportunities for Kai and me to spend time together, now that we were growing up.

"A clock, a watch, can only work one way. If you can

see what that way is, you can fix anything if it breaks."

"I'm glad you like it so much," I said in perfect honesty. "It would make my head hurt and my eyes water."

Kai smiled. He turned his head to look at me, and then his eyes narrowed ever so slightly, as if I was blurry and he was trying to bring me into focus. Lately, I had caught him doing this more and more. There was always an expression in his eyes I couldn't quite decipher.

"I thought you said the sewing already did that," he said at last.

I gave a snort. "You're right. It does."

Over the years, my oma's eyesight had begun to fade. As a result, the fine handiwork that used to fall to her eyes and fingers now fell to mine. The curious thing was that the more I disliked the work, the tinier and more even my stitches had become, until at last I became somewhat famous as a seamstress. Even the ladies in the finest part of town desired my sewing.

Slowly, I had begun to earn enough money so that Oma and I could have moved into a nicer flat, or at least to one on a lower floor. But, by mutual consent, neither Oma nor I ever spoke of such a thing. She did not want to leave her rooftop garden, and I did not want to leave Kai.

"I'm sorry, Grace," Kai said quietly.

Because we knew each other so well, he understood how, as my hands grew more proficient, my spirit struggled. As if the stitches I placed in other people's garments somehow all conspired together to bind me to a life that wasn't what I wanted. Not that I knew what I *did* want, mind you. It's often easier to see what you don't want than what you do. This is a fact of life that I'm hardly the first to have noticed.

"You don't have to be sorry," I answered as we rounded a corner, leaving the shop district behind. We were entering the poorer quarter now, the place where we lived.

"It's not as if it's your fault," I went on. "I'm happy that you like your work, Kai. Honestly, I am."

"I know you are," Kai said. "It's just—"

"I know," I said, cutting him off.

The fact that Kai spent his days doing something that matched his temperament so well, while I did something that matched mine so little, genuinely distressed him. I told myself that this was why he watched me in that close and quiet way of his.

"You could try something else," he suggested now.

"Oh yes?" I answered, my tone short in spite of my best effort. We crossed the street, careful to avoid the horses.

"And just what did you have in mind, taking in laundry or scrubbing floors? Girls don't get apprenticed like boys do, Kai, in case you hadn't noticed. It's not as if I have a lot of options."

I could read and write, which was unusual for a girl from a poor family, but I did not possess any of the other skills that might have made me eligible to work as a governess or a teacher, even if that had been what I'd wanted.

Perhaps if I had seen a clearer vision for my handiwork, I might have dreamed of opening up a shop, of paying others to stitch clothes that I had designed. But I did not. I didn't know quite *what* I wanted. I just knew I was tired of sitting still. There were days when it felt as if my whole body itched to be in motion.

So I headed to the rooftop as often as possible. Even in the dead of winter when I had to bundle up in so many layers that I looked like one of the snowmen the children dressed in cast-off clothes, I went. First thing in the morning, last thing before I went to bed at night, I climbed the stairs from the rooms I shared with my grandmother and clambered out onto the roof.

On the rooftop I could breathe. I could stand in one place and turn in a circle, catching a glimpse of at least some portion of the horizon in whichever direction I sent my eyes. At night, when I could no longer see the shapes of the world around me, I could tilt my gaze upward toward the stars.

On the days when my world felt so small I feared that I would suffocate as Kai's father had so long ago, crushed by the weight of the world itself falling on top of him, standing on the rooftop was the only thing that revived me. On the rooftop I felt free, if only for a few moments.

And then something happened that changed both my life and Kai's forever. My grandmother and his mother died and Kai and I were left alone.

ꕥ ꕥ ꕥ

It was the diphtheria that took them. Regular as clockwork, it came with the thaw each year, as if to make a mockery of the hope that spring should bring. Wrapping bony fingers around unsuspecting throats, and then slowly squeezing the life out of them. Kai's mother fell ill first, and Oma went to nurse her, though both Kai and I urged her to stay at home.

"Your mother has no one else on earth but the three of us, Kai," my grandmother said sternly as we huddled outside the Holmgrens' door. Oma's scarf was tied in a determined bow at her chin. She'd set her hands on her hips and had planted her feet, sure signs that she meant to have her way.

"Neither of you can be spared from your work. That leaves me. There's no sense arguing about it, so you might as well save your breath. Now go out and buy me a chicken so I can make Hannah a nourishing broth."

Kai and I exchanged a glance, and then Kai stepped aside and my grandmother marched through the Holmgrens' front door. Oma did her best to nurse Kai's mother back to health. In addition to the broth, she made a poultice for Frue Holmgren's chest. She kept the fire going day and night to keep her warm. Nothing made any difference. Kai's mother was dead before the month was out. The day Frue Holmgren was buried, my oma took to her bed.

"Grace," she murmured late one night. By now, we both knew that Oma, too, was dying. "I want you to promise me something."

"I will promise anything you like," I said. "Only don't tire yourself."

My oma smiled. She held out a hand, and I slipped mine into it.

Cold, I thought. *She is so very, very cold.* Yet the room around us was so warm that I didn't need the shawl I wore indoors in all but the warmest weather. *It will not be long now,* I thought.

"Promise me that you will use your eyes," my oma said. "Promise me that you will let your heart follow them."

"I will, Oma," I said.

My grandmother squeezed my fingers. "Do one thing more for me, will you?" she asked.

"Anything," I said.

"Tell me a story."

If she'd asked me to stand on my head I could not have been more surprised. Oma always had been the storyteller. I leaned forward, resting my elbows on the bed, one hand still clasping my grandmother's.

"Once upon a time," I began, "there was a brave girl named Grace. . . ."

Oma smiled. All through the night I sat beside her, spinning a tale about a girl who bore my name. And that was how Kai found us the next morning. Sitting together, hands still clasped, but by then my voice had fallen silent and Oma breathed no more.

We buried her in the old graveyard on the hill outside of town, not far from Kai's parents. Beside Oma's headstone were the markers that stood in memory of my father and mother who had been buried far from home. Many in the neighborhood came to pay their respects, but it was the flower vendor, Herre Johannes, who stayed the longest.

"If you need anything, Grace," he said as we stood beside the grave. Herre Johannes turned the soft cap he always wore over and over in his hands. "Your oma and I were always good friends to each other. Don't forget that."

"I won't, Herre Johannes," I said. "Thank you."

Herre Johannes settled the cap back onto his head. He nodded to Kai and to me, then made his way back down the hill. Kai and I stood together, not quite touching.

In the days since Oma's death, a strange awkwardness had fallen between Kai and me. We were on our own now, our lives forever altered by the loss of those we loved. And we were both sixteen, old enough to be considered adults. We had been together, living side by side, for as long as we could remember.

"Let's go home now, Grace," Kai said quietly. "If you want to, you can come back tomorrow."

Without a word, I nodded, turning away from my grandmother's grave. *Which home?* I wondered. *Yours or mine?* Who were Kai and I, how did we fit together, now that those whom we loved were gone?

I had seen Kai watching me, in that quiet way of his, in the days since Oma had died. Several times, I thought he was about to speak, but each time, he held his tongue. But I had a feeling today was the day I would learn what was on his mind.

"Do you think about the future, Grace?" he asked as we walked along.

Spring had come in earnest during Oma's illness. Crocuses bloomed on the hillside. Above our heads, the sky was a perfect arc of deep, rich blue.

"Of course I think about it," I answered, my tone shorter than I intended. I thought about the future all the time. Worried about it was more like it, not that worrying did me any good. Kai stayed silent.

I pulled in a breath and held it, my eyes on the green grass of the hill, the bright, new green that only appears with the first flush of spring as the earth renews itself. I let my breath out slowly and tried again.

"I'm sorry," I said. "I didn't mean to snap. It just seems like kind of a silly question, that's all. Of course I think about the future. What else is there to think about? It scares me."

To my horror, I heard that my voice had dropped to a whisper. I felt the sudden sting of tears at the back of my eyes. All through the days of Oma's illness, through every moment that had followed, I had done my best to overcome this fact. Without success.

"The future terrifies me," I confessed now, my voice rising. "I don't know what to do. I can't see my way, Kai."

"Marry me," said Kai.

FOUR

I abruptly stopped walking.

"*What?*" I cried.

"Marry me," Kai said again. My sudden halt had caught him by surprise. His momentum had carried him several steps along the path, so that now he had to turn around. We faced each other. I saw Kai's own eyes widen in surprise as he caught sight of the astonished expression on my face.

"For heaven's sake, Grace," he said. "You must have thought of this too. It can't be a total surprise. It's the logical next step, and surely it's what my mother and your grandmother always wanted."

"What about what we want?"

Kai's head jerked back, as if I'd struck him. And all of a sudden, I felt more wretched than I ever had in my entire life.

Too fast. It's all happening too fast, I thought.

Quickly, I closed the distance between us, reached out and gripped Kai tightly by the shoulders.

"I spoke without thinking," I said, gazing straight into his eyes. "I did not mean to hurt you. I'm sorry, Kai. Of course I see the sense in what you're saying. It's just . . ."

Kai gazed back, his eyes intent on mine. "It's just that you don't love me enough to marry me," he said.

I tightened my grip further and gave him a shake. "I didn't say that. Did you hear me say that? Stop putting words in my mouth."

I released him and hurried down the hill, my stride just short of a run. *Away. I have to get away,* I thought. Perhaps, if Kai and I hadn't been standing quite so close together, I wouldn't now feel so responsible for the hurt and confusion I'd seen in his face. We'd scrapped, as all children do, quarreling over nonsense. But neither of us had ever really refused the other anything before, not anything important.

"Grace, wait," Kai called. He caught up, matching his pace with mine.

Only someone who understood me as well as Kai did would have done this. Another man might have put a hand on my arm to stop me, at the very least to try and slow me down, but not Kai. He knew it would give me just the opportunity I needed to take the ultimate step: to turn and fight, or to turn and run.

Instead, Kai simply chugged along beside me, the sound of our feet shushing through the new grass. Gradually, my burst of emotion wore itself out and my pace slowed. My exertions had carried us to the bottom of the hill. With just a few more minutes of walking, we would reach the outskirts of town. We would return to our empty rooms.

If I married him, I thought, *I wouldn't have to be alone.* But was that enough to do the thing that Kai was asking? Were holding back fear and trying to prevent loneliness good enough reasons for us to marry, even if they helped us both?

Maybe Kai is right, I thought. *Maybe I don't love him enough.*

"Don't expect me to apologize again," I said without looking at him.

"All right," Kai replied, his tone agreeable. I thought I felt his glance slide in my direction. "Though you know what they say."

"Do I?"

"The third time's the charm."

I felt laughter bubble up inside my chest and decided to let it go. "They do say that, don't they?" I said with a sigh. Kai stayed silent. I turned my head to look at him. "I'm being awful, aren't I?"

"You are," Kai said.

I couldn't quite read his tone. "Thanks for nothing," I said. "I'm trying to apologize."

"Yes," Kai said. "I know you are. You're also trying to get yourself off the hook. Don't think you can fool me, Grace. We know each other too well."

We walked along in silence for a moment. Then, ever so softly, I felt his fingers slide along the inside of my arm until they were laced with mine. It was the first time we'd held hands in a long time.

"I didn't mean to add to your fear, Grace," Kai said quietly.

"You didn't," I protested. "Hey—ow!" At my answer, Kai had squeezed my fingers so hard I thought the bones might crack. "All right, you did scare me, just a little," I admitted.

Kai gave my arm a little shake. "The thing is, Grace," he said, "I don't see why."

"Well, for starters, you might have picked a better place and time."

Kai gave a snort. "All right, I'll give you that," he said. "Though it does make sense, you know. We're both alone now, Grace. If we were to marry—"

"I see that. I honestly do," I interrupted. "It's just . . ."

Both my words and my feet faltered and came to a stop. I looked at Kai. As he always did, he gazed back at me with clear and steady eyes. And suddenly I felt a spurt of irritation, in spite of my best efforts. How could it all look so simple and right from his position, yet so complicated and uncertain from mine?

Our eyes see different things, I thought. *They always have. Even when we're looking in the same direction, standing side by side.*

I let go of his hand. "Is this what you really, truly want, Kai?" I asked. "Is this all?"

A frown burrowed between his eyebrows. "That's a trick question," he said. "I can tell. I just can't see what the trap is yet."

"That's because there isn't one," I said. "I do love you, Kai. I honestly do. And I know our getting married was close to your mother's heart and to my oma's. I guess I always thought we *would* get married some day. I'm just not sure that day can be now."

"Well, I hardly meant today," Kai said, his tone testy.

I gave him a shove. "Stop it," I said. "You know what I mean. Stop pretending that you don't. It doesn't matter that it's the logical next step; it doesn't even matter if it's the step our families would have wanted. What matters is what you and I choose for ourselves."

"All right, I give up," Kai said, throwing up his hands. "What do you choose, Grace? *What is it that you want?*"

"I want to see the world," I burst out. "And I don't mean a glimpse from the rooftop. I want to see more than just the horizon, Kai. I want to see what's beyond it. And if we get married—"

"You think I'll hold you back," he said, his tone strange and flat. "You think I'd try to stop you."

"I don't know what I think," I all but shouted. "What's the matter with you? Can't you see that's just the problem?"

There was a moment's ringing silence. In it, I stared at Kai and he stared back.

If either of us had taken a step, we could have reached out and been in each other's arms. Either one of us could have drawn the other in and held on tight as if we'd never let go. Neither of us moved a muscle. I don't think we'd ever been farther apart than we were in that moment.

"So you don't love me enough to marry me," Kai said.

"I *do* love you enough," I countered. "Just not yet, not now. I want to see what's around the corner first. I want to *do* something. If *you* loved *me*, you'd understand. You'd let me go."

Kai's mouth twisted. "You're making an awfully big assumption, aren't you?"

"What's that?"

"You assume I'll be here when you get back. But I might not be. Who knows? Maybe by the time you finally remember me, I'll have found someone else. I can *do* things too, you know. So don't start thinking I'll be sitting around here *doing nothing* while you're off on your great adventure, because I won't be! Maybe I'll even have an adventure of my own!"

Kai spun away and began to walk toward town, his legs pumping with long and angry strides. I stood where I was, arms at my sides, my hands clenched into fists.

"Fine," I called after Kai's retreating form. "I hope you *do* do something. I hope you *don't* sit around staring at the insides of clocks all your life. And I hope you *do* find someone else! Someone whose heart is so different from yours you have to work the rest of your life to figure out how it works."

As I spoke, I felt the wind come up. A strange

wind. It swirled around my head, lifting my hair as if to tangle it into knots. It traced my face like it wished to commit it to memory. Then, as abruptly as it had come to encircle me, it departed. A moment later, I saw Kai's shirt push flat against his back.

Kai stopped, as if he'd encountered an invisible brick wall. I watched the way his chin lifted, nose scenting the air, head swiveling from side to side. For just one moment, I thought Kai was going to turn back to me. In the next moment, the wind died down. With a shake of his head as if to dispel some errant notion that had caught him unawares, Kai resumed his brisk pace. He didn't look back, not even once.

Just like the Winter Child, I thought suddenly.

And it was only then that I realized what I had done. Like the king in Kai's favorite tale, I had uttered a wish and a curse combined.

That night, I dreamed of loss.

I was in a strange country, walking through an unfamiliar landscape. My heart pounded in my chest and a fine, cold sweat seemed to cover every inch of my skin. I was searching for something, searching for Kai.

There were times when I could see his outline in the distance, hear his voice drifting back to me on a wind I thought I recognized. The wind from the afternoon—the one that had come up, as if from nowhere, to scuttle between me and Kai.

Wind of change, I thought.

But no matter how I strained my ears to listen to the sound of Kai's voice, I could not understand what he was saying. Was he calling for me, asking me to follow him? Or was he trying to drive me away, demanding I turn back and leave him alone?

Did he love me as he always had? Or had my words driven a wedge between us, opening a gap wider than the one that separated our buildings, a space not even I would be brave enough to cross?

"Kai! Kai, wait for me," I called. I saw his head turn toward me, gazing over his shoulder. Just for an instant, his eyes met mine.

In the next second, he turned away, and I saw for the first time the dark expanse in front of him, reaching out from side to side like a pair of outstretched arms. The chasm was so wide that I could not see across it.

"Kai, wait for me!" I called once more. "Kai, no!"

But I was too late. I watched as Kai raised a leg and stepped out into the open space. Between one of my horrified heartbeats and the next, he was gone.

I sat up in bed, my heart a bright pain inside my chest. My gasping breaths showed white in the air. *Cold,* I thought. *How can it be so cold?* Just that afternoon, it had been spring. Now, as I looked toward the window, I could see a thin etching of frost on the outside of the glass.

I began to shiver. *It's a late storm,* I thought. *This is nothing more than Winter trying to have the last word, the same as it does every year.* Surely I had experienced such late storms before. But even as I tried to reassure myself, I knew it wasn't true. This was not some late-season frost. The cold I felt was something much, much more.

I threw back the covers and got out of bed, hissing between my teeth as my feet hit the icy floor. I dashed to the window, undid the fastening, and pushed it open. Frigid air flowed in to wrap me in its cold embrace. A bright moon floated in the sky overhead. By its light, I could see that Kai's window was wide open. The street below me sparkled with hoarfrost. In the rime, I could see a single set of footprints leaving Kai's building and heading down the street.

I don't remember putting on my stockings and shoes. Don't remember throwing my winter cloak around my shoulders. What I remember clearly is standing in the street, gazing down that straight line of footsteps. It led to the corner, then turned, vanishing from sight.

Gone. My heart thundered in my chest. *Gone. Gone. Gone.*

It did no good for my mind to assert that Kai was safe in bed, for it to reason with me that the footprints could belong to anyone. My heart knew the truth.

Kai was gone. He had followed the Winter Child.

Five

Story the Third

Enter the Winter Child

I am never cold.

Cold's absence is my first clear memory, as clear as the stars on a frosty winter's night. Clear as the way a voice can carry over an expanse of pristine snow in the still, predawn air. And with this memory comes understanding:

I am not like other girls.

Well, of course not.

You were never going to be like other girls anyway, you're tempted to say. I am a princess, after all. But there's not a princess on the planet with my attributes. Many may be called upon to keep the peace and to settle treaties by marrying some prince they've never seen. Others may labor under enchantment, twiddling their thumbs in boredom until some fellow on a white horse, or a horse of any color for that matter, rides up to break the spell.

But I defy you to find another princess who can do what I can, what I must: right a wrong she did not commit. Mend hearts too numerous to count with a single icy touch.

"Why me?" I used to ask my father over and over, and with such regularity that I'm sure he could have set his watch by the question. "Why did the North Wind choose me and not someone else? Why must *I* be a Winter Child?"

The answer, which my father never failed to give despite the way it must have pained him, was as plain as the nose on my face. A face that was much like the face of another—one whom Papa never spoke of if he could help it.

"Because of your mother," he always replied.

I knew the story, of course, though not from Papa. Not from any one person at all, in fact, but rather from everyone—and everything—around me.

There wasn't a person in my father's kingdom who didn't know the tale of what had happened, the details of how I had become a Winter Child. Nor did the knowledge end there. Every tree, every rock, every flower that bloomed and every frost that killed it knew the tale as well. The story was so much a part of the fabric of my father's kingdom that it was in the water we drank, the air we breathed, the first flush of green that came in spring, the last winter snowfall.

Speaking the details was simply unnecessary. Each time I was laced into a dress for some fancy court occasion, I felt it in the way my ladies in waiting worked hard not to let their fingertips touch my skin.

So cold, and she can't feel a thing. It's unnatural, but what can you expect? She is a Winter Child.

I felt it in the way the castle servants turned their backs each time I snuck out of the castle dressed in a set of the head cook's youngest son's outgrown clothes.

Another princess would never be allowed to get away with such a thing, but then we must make allowances for her, mustn't we? Her time for fun and games will end soon enough—and then just think of what comes next.

Poor little Deirdre. Poor little Winter Child.

It isn't easy being different, let me tell you. But it's even more challenging to be different in a way that's so obvious nobody ever feels the need to acknowledge it. An obvious that is so well-established you can almost fool yourself into believing it's going overlooked.

Almost.

"Then why didn't the North Wind just take my mother instead?" I would ask my father.

One particular interrogation occurred when I was eight years old. Halfway to the milestone of sixteen, the year in which I would be called to fulfill the destiny *she* had mapped out for me.

She. Her. My mother. I'd never called her by her given name. I couldn't. I didn't know what it was. Though I'd pestered my father with a million other questions, this was one I'd never dared to ask.

"If the North Wind wanted her attention so much, why didn't it just snatch *her* up in its arms?"

"You know I don't have an answer to that question, Deirdre," my father said. "It was the North Wind's choice, not mine."

"But I *want* you to have the answer, Papa!" I said, restraining the desire to stamp my foot with momentous effort. Such behavior might be acceptable at six, but never in an eight-year-old. "You're a king. You should have an answer for everything."

A strange expression came over my father's face, as if two factions were battling for possession of it. On the one hand, he looked sad and weary. On the other, it seemed that he wanted to smile. Before the matter could be settled, my father held out his arms. I crawled into them, settling into his lap with my head against his shoulder. He rested his chin on the top of my head. I couldn't see him do it, but I was pretty sure my father closed his eyes.

"I want you to listen to me, my daughter," he said. "What I am going to say may not make much sense to you now, but you will understand as you grow older."

I squirmed a little, in spite of the comfort of my father's embrace. Nobody likes to be told they're not old enough to grasp something important.

"I'm eight," I remarked. Halfway to the sixteen years I would need to possess in order to set out on what I was already sarcastically referring to as "my great quest."

"I know how old you are, Deirdre," my father replied, and I thought I caught a hint of laughter in his tone. This was enough to stop my squirming in an instant. My father didn't laugh very often. He hardly even smiled.

"I was there the moment you were born, when you had all the possibilities of the world before you. That person is still there, inside you. The North Wind's embrace has not changed that. It has not changed who you truly are."

"But you gave me a Winter Child's name," I said. "You called me 'Sorrow.'"

"Only to prepare you for what would lie ahead," replied my father. "You must learn patience, Little One."

"Maybe you should have named me that instead," I interrupted, and this time, I felt a tremor of what I was sure was laughter shimmy through my father's body.

"Perhaps you're right about that," he said, giving me a quick squeeze. "But listen to me now. When your task is complete, you may choose a name for yourself, the one you desire above all others. On that day, your life will begin anew. It will be as if you have been reborn."

I twisted in my father's lap so that I could look into his eyes.

If my first memory is of being cold, my second is of my father's eyes. They were a deep and piercing green, like the needles of the evergreens that grow in the woods that mark the boundary between our kingdom and the lands beyond my father's realm.

Always, it seems to me that I feel my father's gaze, even now that death has closed his eyes. Watching over me with love and concern, promising that, in the end, I will find the way to solve the puzzle of my own existence, to right all the wrongs not of my own creation and, at the last, even find the means to mend my own wounded heart.

"I can choose my own name?"

"Absolutely," my father vowed. "You were not born to be called Sorrow."

His eyes kindled now with a bright green flame. "Just think, Deirdre," he went on. "You have a chance almost no one else is granted. The opportunity to choose your own name, one to match who you truly are inside."

"But how will I know what to choose?" I asked.

"Excellent question," my father replied. "All I can tell you is that you will know when the time comes. In the meantime . . ."

My father's eyes began to sparkle with laughter, which always made my heart sing with joy.

"We could start to compile a list of possibilities," he said. Making lists was something my father did a lot. It could be because he was a king or just because that's who he was. I've never quite been able to sort this out.

"Ermyntrude, for instance. Now *there's* a name to be reckoned with," my father went on. "Three syllables, a nice round name. And I'll bet you wouldn't have to share it with too many other girls."

My father paused and raised his eyebrows. If the game were to continue, it was now up to me.

"What about Hortensia?" I proposed. "That has four syllables."

My father nodded, as if I'd made a very astute

point. "Esmerelda," he said. "Also four. Or what about Gudrun? Only two, but when I was a lad it was very popular. Gudrun is a name with staying power."

"Penelope is nice," I said.

"Zahalia," my father countered.

"Oh, Papa, I know," I suddenly exclaimed. "Brunhilde. I should have thought of it before. 'Brunhilde' is a name that always gets a reaction."

To my surprise and dismay, it got a reaction from my father I hadn't anticipated. He made a face, as if he'd tasted something sour. I watched as the laughter faded from his face, and the sadness moved to the front of his green eyes once more.

"Your mother had a cousin named Brunhilde," he said. "She was the maid of honor at our wedding."

And just like that, the game was done.

"I'm sorry, Papa," I said quietly. "I didn't know."

My father reached out to twist the end of one of my pale locks around his finger, and then he gave it a tug.

"Of course you didn't, Little One," he said. "So you've nothing to be sorry for." He lifted me from his lap, set me on my feet, and then stood up.

For a moment, I thought he would say something more. That at last he would speak of her, my mother, his wife, the woman who had changed the course of both our lives. But he did not. Mine was the heart with ice inside it, but even as a child I knew my father's heart carried a wound far greater than mine. A wound that was beyond even my power to heal, a wound he would carry into the grave itself.

"I should get back to my study," my father announced. He bent to give me a kiss, then turned to go. "Speaking of names, I need to review the list of all the foreign ambassadors I'm going to meet tomorrow, and then I'll have to remember to ask Dominic to . . ."

Dominic was my father's steward, his right-hand man. I could tell from the sound of Papa's voice that his thoughts had already traveled far ahead of his body. I could only hope he would forgive me for calling them back.

"Papa," I burst out, after he'd gone no more than a dozen steps. "Come back. I have to ask you something."

"Gracious, Deirdre," my father said, snapping back to the present and turning around quickly at the fierceness of my tone. "What on earth is the matter, Little One?"

"It's her name, my mother's name," I said, and with that, I suddenly discovered I was crying. "I have to know it, don't you see? So I don't add it to the list by accident. I don't want her name. I don't want to be like she was."

"Deirdre," my father said.

I think that was the moment when I grew up, for in the two syllables of my own name I suddenly heard and understood something I previously had not. My father hadn't just bestowed the name of Sorrow on me. He'd also bestowed it on himself.

"Joy," my father said. "Your mother's name was Joy."

Then he turned and walked away. This was the last time we spoke about her.

Six

Though my father and I never discussed names again, that afternoon marked the beginning of my fascination with them. I began to make a study of names, collecting them much like other children collected coins or stamps or dolls.

It wasn't simply the sound of a name that appealed to me, though I did enjoy this: the way a name felt inside your mouth as you formed its syllables, the space it occupied in the air when you pronounced it. But there was also the way a name and the person who bore it got along together. For this, or so it always seemed to me, was the heart of what a name is all about.

Was the fit between a name and its bearer seamless and comfortable? The castle baker was called Amelia, for instance, a name that seemed to suit her quite well. It sounded soft coming and going, like a flourish of icing on a fancy cake, but in the center there was a core of strength, the press of bread being kneaded against its board. A*mel*ia.

Or did the name sit uncomfortably upon its wearer, did it chafe and rub? My father's steward could enter a room so soundlessly you'd never know he was there until he cleared his throat. Yet he was called Dominic, a name that always sounded to me like the sharp clatter of heels along a hall of flagstones.

Had Dominic known his name did not suit him and deliberately set out to cultivate a set of traits to counterbalance this? Did his name cause him discomfort? Did moving silently help to ease this pain? Did we grow into our names, and if so, could we grow out of them? Did we shape them, or did they shape us?

The names that interested me the most were the ones that belonged to people who paid them no attention at all. The people who carried their names around like sacks on their backs, never really recognizing the power of the name they bore. Such an interest was hardly surprising, I suppose. Did I not carry the name Sorrow all because my mother had overlooked the power of her own name and forgotten that she was named Joy?

And so I quietly continued my pursuit of names as the years pursued me, until at last, the day of my sixteenth birthday arrived.

You know what happened already, of course. How I dressed myself in a gown of finest linen, sheer as gossamer. Upon my feet I wore a pair of crystal boots.

But what the stories never remember is that it was my father who put the staff of ash wood into my hand. It was he who threw the snow-white cloak around my shoulders.

The stories also fail to share that Amelia baked me the largest cake anyone had ever seen, the inside as dark and rich as fertile earth with an outside covered in snow-white icing. It was so large there was enough for every single person in the kingdom to have a piece, so sweet it brought a tear to each and every eye.

The stories fail to tell how, after eating their pieces of cake in celebration of my birth, the people of my father's kingdom faded away, like snow upon warm ground, until only my father and I were left—the king and his daughter, the princess, the Winter Child, standing outside the gates of our ice palace. My father fussed a little with the lacings of my cloak, tying the strings so that they lay tight against the base of my throat.

"Papa," I said, astonished I could speak with the lump that filled my throat, a lump made up of all the things I feared I had forgotten to say but would never have the chance to now.

"I don't even need a cloak. I'm never cold. Please, stop fussing."

"I'd like you to wear one anyway," my father answered. He tweaked the cloak, adjusting it so that it hung perfectly straight from my shoulders. "Neither of us knows how long a road you must travel, Little One. A cloak may be useful along the way."

After all these years, he still called me Little One, the nickname he'd given me as a child so that neither of us would have to spend our days listening to him call me Sorrow.

"There may be days when your heart feels cold, though your body does not. On those days, it will be good to have something to draw in close around you."

"And this?" I asked, gesturing to the staff of ash wood he'd placed into my hand.

"So that you can imagine I am with you on your journey," my father said at once. "And when you need to, you can lean upon me."

Suddenly, I found it almost impossible to breathe.

"I don't want to," I choked out. "I don't want any of this. I don't want to leave you, Papa."

"Ah, Deirdre," my father said, drawing me into his arms.

For sixteen years I had been so careful never to speak those words. I might have asked a thousand questions about it, but not once had I truly railed against the fate my father and I both knew could not be avoided. But standing with my father before the gates of the palace on my sixteenth birthday, I could hold in my true feelings no longer.

I did not want to leave. I did not want to be a Winter Child.

The thought of mending all those hearts was daunting enough, but there was something more, a sorrow that would come to my father and me alone. I would not change. From the moment I set out to fulfill my Winter Child's destiny, I would not grow one day older until my task was done.

But my father was as mortal as the rest of the world was. He would continue to age, to feel the passage of time. Once I left him to set out on my journey, I would never see him again, not in any way that felt familiar to me now. His mortal life would be over before my task was complete.

"If I could have spared us the pain of this parting, I would have," my father said. "But there's no way to do it. There hasn't been since the day the North Wind first snatched you up in its arms. A parting of this nature would have come upon us even if you had not been called to be a Winter Child, Deirdre. It comes to all parents and children, to all who truly love."

"If you're trying to make me feel better, it isn't working," I managed to say.

And suddenly, my father laughed, a bright, clear sound. It seemed to carry on the cold air, as if setting out ahead of me. And I knew that, somewhere along my journey, I would remember that even in our moment of greatest sadness, I had made my father laugh.

"I want you to listen to me now," my father went on. "This is going to be a lecture, so pay close attention."

I couldn't quite manage a laugh, but I attempted a smile.

"I'm listening," I promised.

"The world is full of change, Deirdre," he told me. "That is its nature, for the very globe itself spins around. It is never still—always moving, therefore always changing. Today is the day that the curve of the earth will catch us in its spin and whirl us apart. But I will never truly leave you, just as you will never leave me."

My father placed a hand on the center of his chest. Suddenly understanding, I reached to cover his hand with one of mine. And so we stood together with our hands pressed against his heart.

"You will be inside my heart," my father said, "just as I will be in yours. Even when my heart ceases to beat, I will be with you. You will never be alone and neither will I."

How I wanted to be brave!

"But it won't be the same," I whispered.

"No," my father answered simply. "It will not. Nothing stays the same, Deirdre. That, too, is part of life. Sometimes, pushing against change only makes it push back twice as hard. But even the most bitter fruit may contain something sweet at its core. A taste you would never have encountered if you had not been willing to endure the bitter first."

He looked at me, his green eyes steady. I held my breath, waiting for him to say more. But it had never been my father's way to offer more words than were needed, just as it was not his way to offer false comfort. And so I knew that the next words spoken would not be his; they would be mine.

"I can do it, Papa," I promised.

And then, finally, I saw the bright sheen of tears in my father's eyes.

"I know you can," he said. "I have never doubted that."

"That doesn't mean I'm going to like it," I went on.

"I'll tell you a secret," my father said. "I've never cared for it very much myself."

The sound of my heart beating was loud in my ears. I could feel the winter sun on my back, even as the cold air stung my nostrils. A bird called in the sky overhead, and another answered from far off. A small wind, a curious wind, suddenly arrived to investigate the hem of my cloak. My father and I did not move. But I felt the world begin to shift and turn around me. The path that I must follow was unfurling at my back.

"So," I said.

"So," my father echoed.

And with that, I took a single step back. I felt a quick, hard pain spear my heart. I saw a spasm shoot across my father's face, and I knew he felt the same pain.

"I love you, Papa," I said.

"And I love you," my father replied. "I have loved you every day of your life. I will love you for every day of mine and more. My love will never diminish, no matter how many steps you take throughout the world, no matter how many years you wander until your task is done."

"I will love you as long as I draw breath," I replied. "And the moment I stop breathing, I will find you. Wherever you are."

"I will be waiting for you with open arms," my father said.

I took a second step back, and then a third and a fourth. With each and every step I took, I felt my heart give a painful tug. It seemed to me that I could almost see what caused it: the invisible line that connected my father's heart to mine. Thin as spider's silk, incredibly strong. It would stretch between us always, winding around the earth like a map of my wanderings. Never breaking, never releasing its hold.

"Don't look back when you turn to go," my father said. "Set your face to the path and keep on going. Will you do this for me?"

"Only if you'll do the same," I said. "Please don't stand here and watch me walk away from you."

"On the count of three, then," my father said.

"No, five," I said quickly. "Make it five, Papa."

I saw my father smile for the very last time.

"Five, then," said my father. "Are you ready?"

"No," I answered with a shaky laugh. "But you can start counting anyhow."

"One," my father said, as his eyes stayed steadily on mine. I gripped the staff of ash wood tightly in my right hand, feeling every groove, every whorl. Trying to ignore the fact that my palm was slick with sweat in spite of the coldness of the day.

"Two," said my father. "Three." I heard the soft *shush* as a nearby tree branch let go of its burden of snow and it fell wetly to the ground.

"Four." My stomach muscles tightened. Just one

count more. One syllable, and I would turn away from my father forever.

"Five," my father said softly.

At that moment, the wind snuck beneath my cloak and tugged it out behind me. The lacings pulled against my throat.

No! my heart cried. *Not now. Not yet. Not ever.*

But even as my heart protested, my mind accepted the truth. I did not have a choice. Again the wind tugged, and this time, I let it turn me. The pain in my heart was so sharp I thought it would surely split in two.

Through my pain, I heard the scrape of my father's boot heel. I knew that he had kept his promise. This was what finally gave me the courage to take a step. My first upon my quest as a Winter Child.

Away from the palace made of snow and ice I walked, away from all I knew and loved. The wind was like a guiding hand at the small of my back, as if to make sure I would keep going.

SEVEN

Story the Fourth

In Which Some Paths Cross and Others Merely Walk Side by Side

How long did I wander? How many hearts did I meet, how many hearts did I mend before I encountered Grace and Kai? Good questions, all. The trouble is, I can't answer them.

It will help if you remember that I have a somewhat unusual relationship with time.

I was on my journey, fulfilling my quest, performing my duties as a Winter Child. As long as I did this, I would not age. I would stay precisely as I was.

Therefore, keeping track of time served no purpose. Some years felt long, other years felt short. They weren't what mattered anyway. What mattered were the hearts I found and mended, one by one.

I can tell you that by the time the wind, who was my only companion, brought me the sound of the name "Grace," I had crossed the world and recrossed it many times in my journey as a Winter Child. Along with my age, my interest in names remained constant. The longer I journeyed, the more hearts I encountered, and the more I began to see a pattern forming:

Those whose names fit them least on the outside often were the ones who carried a wounded heart on the inside.

Occasionally, though only very rarely, I also came across someone else: a person whose inside and outside were such a perfect match they almost had the power to mend hearts themselves. So is it any wonder that, when the wind brought me the sound of a girl named "Grace," I hurried to see what she looked like?

Grace.

What a lovely possibility-filled name. Possibility for generosity, for forgiveness. If there was an opposite to Sorrow, it seemed Grace just might be it. So I hurried to see her, following the wind, and discovered that this Grace was not alone. She had a young man with her, and even eyes much less perceptive than mine could have seen that these two were in the midst of a quarrel.

Most people can't see me. The tales told about me say that this is because I'm not meant to be seen by ordinary eyes. The truth is slightly different, I think: I'm not intended to be seen by ordinary hearts.

Nevertheless, over the years I have learned to be careful, learned it's best to keep out of sight. Sudden revelations that bedtime stories might actually be real are unsettling, to say the least. I'm here to mend hearts, not to stop them with fright.

For obvious reasons, it's easiest for me to conceal myself when the world around me contains a lot of snow or ice, but even on a warm summer's day I can usually find a pocket of air in which to hide. The trouble with being concealed, of course, is that sometimes you witness events you wish you hadn't. This is precisely what happened with Grace and Kai.

That was his name, the young man with her. Kai—to rhyme with sigh. And Grace was giving him plenty to sigh about, I soon discovered.

With both hands, Grace was pushing away love.

I don't get angry very often. There's just no purpose in it. Getting mad about something usually makes whatever caused your anger in the first place even worse. But the sight, the sound, of what was happening between these two made me angry, angrier than I'd been in a good long while. Angrier than I could ever remember being, in fact.

Grace was doing two things no one ever should: She was denying the possibilities of her name, and she was denying the potential of love.

Gently putting love aside is one thing. None of us can accept all of what we may be offered in this life. Sometimes we must say no, even to love.

But this girl named Grace was pushing love away with both hands, arms straight out in front of her, elbows locked. With all the force of her being, she was pushing away a great gift, and the worst thing of all was that it seemed to me she was doing it without truly consulting her heart.

Oh, she thought she was. She thought she was doing just what her heart wanted. Her words made that clear enough. But with a name like Sorrow, I can always spot it in another. I have to. It's part of my job.

And so I knew that this girl, this Grace, had sorrow and pain and fear in her heart, and I also knew she was denying they were there just as fiercely as she was refusing love. In spite of all her words about freedom, her heart was bound.

You are just like my mother, Grace, I thought. A name and a heart so at odds that one could not find the other.

And with this realization, I felt my anger fade. I watched as the argument reached its conclusion and the young man spun on one heel and set off for home. The wind hurried after, barely taking the time to swirl around Grace before dashing against Kai, plastering the shirt he wore against his back.

He stopped, and my heart began to beat so hard and fast the sound of it rang in my ears. I watched as Kai's head turned quickly from side to side, as if hoping to catch a glimpse of something he was sure was there but could not quite see.

And suddenly, I was dizzy. Possible paths opened before me only to splinter and then re-form like the colorful pieces of a kaleidoscope. That was the moment I understood, even as Kai was hunching his shoulders against the wind and continuing to walk. As Grace was standing alone, her expression stricken and desolate as she watched him.

The three of us were not finished with one another. Not by a long shot. We all had a very long way to go.

Eight

I waited until the middle of the night. When the world grows still and the hearts of dreamers lie wide open. This is when I do most of my work.

Most people never even know I've touched their hearts. They simply wake up the next morning feeling better than they had when they closed their eyes the previous night. Usually, it's only after many such mornings have come and gone that those whose hearts I've mended recognize there's anything different about themselves. Even then, they might not be able to tell you what it is.

It isn't happiness, not quite yet. Instead, it's a lessening of that for which I am named, a lessening of sorrow. It is the creation of a space so that something else can come and take sorrow's place, the thing for which my mother was named but which she could not find within herself. I create a space for joy.

Every once in a while, though, I encounter someone who can truly see me. Not just the traces that I leave behind, like the frost on the windowpane that children are taught denotes my presence. I mean my actual form. There's a reason for this, I think: These are the hearts that have been willing to believe I exist, against all logical odds.

I've only met a handful of them during my journey, but each and every one holds a special place in my heart. For it is these hearts that have schooled my own to hope. They remind me to hold fast to the belief that there is a heart that can help me mend my own.

Standing in the narrow street that divided Grace's tall building from Kai's, I gazed at her dark windows high above. The full moon that had been playing hide-and-seek among the buildings abruptly gave up the game and leaped over the rooftops to hang like a great white plate in the sky. The street around me was flooded with its pale light.

Nothing ventured, nothing gained, I thought.

I turned and directed my upward gaze toward Kai's windows. Like Grace's, his were dark. Sensible people were asleep, even if what they dreamed wasn't sensible at all.

What do you dream, Kai? I wondered. He'd come so close to seeing me that afternoon. Dared I hope his dreams were of the Winter Child?

I spread my arms. Instantly, the wind appeared, filling my cloak. Up, up, up into the air the wind carried me, until I could place my hands against Kai's windows.

Beneath my palms, the panes of glass grew cold. I knew this because I could see a thin film of ice begin to form, spreading out, then cracking like sweet sugar glaze.

Wake up, Kai, I thought. *Wake up!* And then the window opened and I was looking straight into Kai's eyes. They were blue. I could see this by the light of the moon. Not a pale blue such as mine, but the deep blue of an alpine lake after the sun has gone down behind the mountains. They gazed out steadily, though the expression in them was startled. I could hardly blame him for that. It's not every day you literally come face-to-face with someone straight out of a fairy tale.

When I spoke, his eyes widened. "Hello," I said.

"Hello," he replied. His voice was quiet and steady, the kind of voice made for making promises. Then, just like that, Kai's eyes narrowed, as if the light of the moon had grown too strong for him.

"How do you do that?" he blurted out. And I discovered that even a girl named Sorrow can still smile. It was a reasonable question. He did live on the top floor. It just wasn't the question I'd been expecting.

"I can do anything," I boasted. "I'm a Winter Child."

He shook his head in a quick, determined motion of contradiction. "No," he said. "That isn't right."

I lifted my chin, as if in defiance, though, as it had that afternoon, I could feel my heart begin to pound. "What can't I do?" I asked.

"You know the answer to that as well as I do," Kai replied without hesitation. "You cannot heal your own heart."

I felt a sharp pain as my heart contracted, then expanded, opening wider than it had known how to until this moment.

"Can you do it?" I asked. "Are you the one who can heal my heart?"

Kai looked at me for several moments, his eyes still narrowed in a slightly unsettling way. It was as if he thought he could figure out the way I was put together, how I worked, if only he could stare at me long enough. Again, my heart felt a painful, hopeful pang. If someone can see the way something works, they can see how to fix it when it breaks, can't they? Wasn't this precisely what I did myself?

"I don't know," Kai finally said. His voice was troubled. "Is that why I can see you, because you want me to try?"

"You can see me because you believe in me," I answered.

He gave another quick shake of his head.

"No," he said. "There's something more. It's because *you* believe in *me* that I can see you, isn't it? And because *I* want to try. I always have, I think, from the time I first heard your story when I was just a boy.

"I always knew there was more to the tale than just being a bedtime story. I knew that you were just as real as I was."

"And so I am," I said.

He smiled then, and I felt my own lips curve up in answer. "Yes," he said. "I see that you are."

My heart had become a rushing river. *So this is*

what it feels like to hope, I thought. *It makes you light-headed, and sets all your limbs to trembling with strength and weakness combined.*

"And my heart?" I asked, amazed to hear my voice come out just as steady as his. "Do you want to try and heal it?"

"I think I must," Kai answered slowly, as if the admission were welling up from someplace deep inside him. His eyes slid from mine to fix on something just over my right shoulder. At first I thought it must be Grace's window, but when he spoke again, I realized I'd been wrong.

"I used to ask about your heart," he went on softly, "when Grace's oma would tell us your story. It always seemed so unfair to me, to give you the power to heal so many hearts but not enough to heal your own."

The past. He is looking at the past, I thought. *The past that has made him what he is now.* A past that would give me a chance for a future. We stood in silence for several minutes. I gazed at Kai. He gazed at his former self. With an effort I could almost feel inside my own body, Kai shifted his eyes back to me.

"Where must we go?"

I pulled in a breath before I spoke. "Just like that?"

He made a sound that reached toward laughter. "Well, hardly. I *have* been hearing your story my whole life."

"Don't you dare ask me how old I really am."

This time, Kai did laugh. "I wouldn't dream of it,"

he promised. "Besides, I already know. Grace's oma used to say that you would stay the same age until your quest was done. You're sixteen, just like Grace and I are."

"Very cleverly answered," I replied. "So what makes you think we have to go anywhere? Why can't we settle things right here and now? Perhaps all you need to do is kiss me and be done with it."

"I'm not a prince," Kai said. "I think that only works for them. Besides . . ."

He drew the second syllable out, as if he were formulating his answer even as he spoke. "Having an answer as simple as a kiss wouldn't make sense. It wouldn't fit with the rest of the tale. You're on a journey, a quest, in search of all those other wounded hearts. So I think a journey must be the way to heal your heart as well.

"In which case I'll repeat the question. Where must we go?"

That was the moment when I realized how very much I wished to be in love.

Certainly it was the moment that I felt the future begin to open up before me, as my heart had opened itself to hope just a few minutes before. Perhaps love and hope are one and the same. I don't know. I do know this was the moment when the future ceased to be a desolate place, a place where I would always walk alone. By the use of a single pronoun, one simple "we," Kai had created a path where two might walk side by side.

If I was very lucky, the two might even hold hands. I extended mine.

"Home," I said. "We're going home."

I hadn't known what the answer was until I spoke. But now that I had, I knew it was right. *Home.* Back to the place where my strange journey had begun.

"I'll come with you," Kai said. "But I'm not going out through the window, if you don't mind. I don't think I'm ready to fly through the air. I'm just a mortal who likes to keep his feet on the ground."

"Suit yourself," I said. "Though you don't know what you're missing. I warn you—someday I hope to change your mind."

He turned from the window.

"Kai."

He turned back. "What?"

"Will you tell her good-bye?"

If Kai was surprised by my question, he didn't show it. Nor did he ask whom I was talking about.

"No," he said after a moment. He gazed past my shoulder, as he had done earlier. I knew he was thinking of Grace this time.

"I don't think so. There isn't any point. I used to think we'd always understand each other, that we would always walk the same path. I don't think that anymore."

His eyes shifted. Now they looked straight into mine. "I'm going to walk a new path," he said, "and see where it takes me."

"I'm glad," I said.

"So am I."

And that is how it came to pass that Kai left

his warm bed and all he had once held dear, and he embarked upon a journey with no milestones to guide him. A single line of footprints in an unseasonably late frost was all that remained to mark his departure.

Kai did not look back. So, just as he turned the corner at the end of the street, when he could not see me do it, I looked back for him. My gaze went straight to the rooftop of Grace's building, with her darkened windows just beneath.

What will you do when you discover Kai is gone? I wondered. *Will you find a way to follow? Or will you give in to pride and let him go?*

I found the courage to venture my heart, Grace. Now let's see if you have the courage to venture yours.

Nine

Story the Fifth

In Which Grace Makes a Choice

He was gone. Kai was gone. He had followed the Winter Child.

I stood in the street, staring down the trail his footprints had left in the frost until I could no longer feel my feet and the hem of my nightgown was soaked. Until I could hear Oma's voice in my mind, clear as a bell:

For heaven's sake, Grace, get back inside this minute before you catch your death of cold.

Though I never catch cold.

It's the strangest thing. Not even Oma could account for it, which meant the familiar scolding was also something of a joke. But suddenly, catching cold was precisely what I feared. I feared my luck might run out just when I needed it most.

Kai had asked me to marry him, and I had turned him away. I had turned him away and now he was gone.

Oh, Grace, I thought as I finally began to shiver. *What have you done?*

It took all day to sort out my affairs. Unlike Kai, I didn't simply walk out and leave everything behind me. There was the landlord to speak to, completed work to send to my patrons, and incomplete work for which I needed to make arrangements for others to finish.

"I'd feel better about all this if I knew when you were coming back, Grace," the flower vendor, Herre Johannes, said late that afternoon.

He and I were standing together on the rooftop, *my* rooftop, among Oma's pots and planters. It was still too cold to sow seeds, but I had turned the soil over on the first clear day in preparation for when it would grow warm enough.

I had given Herre Johannes all of the notes that Oma and I had made about what should be planted where, and I was sure the old flower vendor would have some thoughts of his own. He was moving into my old rooms and would care for the rooftop garden in my absence. This suited both Herre Johannes and my landlord well.

Oma's garden had made our building famous. My landlord never lacked for tenants, even when times were hard. Standing on the rooftop now, I felt my first pang of regret. The rooftop garden was the one thing I would be sorry to leave behind.

"I'd be happier if I knew where you were going," Herre Johannes continued.

"That makes two of us," I said. I caught the worried expression on Herre Johannes's kind and wrinkled face and bit down on the tip of my tongue.

I am going to miss him, too, I thought. Strangely, it made me feel better to know that I would miss not simply a place, which could not miss me back, but a living, beating heart of flesh and blood.

I placed what I hoped was a comforting hand on Herre Johannes's arm.

"I spoke without thinking, Herre Johannes," I said. "I'm sorry. I have thought about what I'm doing, honestly."

But I hadn't been truthful with Herre Johannes, not entirely. I'd let him believe the obvious, that Kai had gone off in a huff following a sweethearts' quarrel. I kept to myself the knowledge that he'd actually chosen to do something much more dangerous and difficult than that: He was walking the path of the Winter Child.

Herre Johannes reached to give my hand a pat, and I dropped my arm. He rubbed one set of knuckles against the stubble on his chin. It made a rough and scratchy sound.

"You've been dreaming of striking out into the world for a good long while, I think," he said.

It was all I could do to keep my mouth from dropping open. Something of my struggle must have shown in my face, for Herre Johannes gave a chuckle. I laughed too, as I shook my head.

"Was it so obvious?"

"To someone who sees only the outside of you,

no," he answered promptly. "But for anyone able to catch a glimpse of the inside of you . . ."

He broke off for a moment, gazing over my shoulder. It came to me suddenly that Herre Johannes was doing what I always had done when I came to the rooftop: He was gazing into the distance, his eyes seeking out the horizon.

"I have known you for a long time, Grace," he said. "I have watched you grow up, and your grandmother and I were good friends. I think, sometimes, that you are like the plants in her garden, always turning your face toward the sun.

"But I want you to remember something," Herre Johannes said, his eyes on my face now. "A plant needs to do more than stretch its leaves toward the sun. It also needs to send down roots deep into the ground. They hold on tightly in the dark, out of sight where it is easy to forget about them. But it is the fact that a plant can do these two things at once, anchoring itself to the earth even as it reaches for the sky, that makes it strong.

"If the roots fail, the plant will die every time. Do you understand what I am trying to say?"

"I think so." I nodded. "You are trying to remind me not to get so consumed in what lies ahead that I forget about where I came from. You want me to remember to look both forward and back."

"There now," Herre Johannes said, and he pressed a kiss to my forehead. "Your grandmother was right. She always said you were a smart one."

Not smart enough to keep Kai from leaving, I thought. *Not smart enough to truly see him even though he's spent his whole life standing at my side. Not so smart that I stopped myself from driving him away, straight into the arms of the Winter Child.*

But I did not say these things aloud. "I will never be as smart as you are," I said as I put my arms around Herre Johannes and held on tight.

Herre Johannes made a rumbling sound deep in his chest. "Yes, well," he said. "It helps if you remember that I am very old."

"And your roots are strong," I said as I let him go. I stepped back, the better to see his face in the fading light.

"As are yours," Herre Johannes replied. "Remember that, when your journey seems difficult. Remember that I will be thinking of you as I tend the garden."

"I will," I promised.

We left the rooftop just as the sun went down.

Ten

Story the Sixth

In Which Kai Finally Finds His Voice

I suppose you're wondering why I haven't said anything until now.

If Grace were here she'd tell you I don't talk all that much, not unless I really have something to say, anyhow. Which makes me sound like some strong and silent type. Totally untrue, of course. And Grace isn't here. That's part of the point. If the two of us hadn't quarreled, if we'd stayed together, neither of us would have much of a story to tell. Or at the very least, they would be different from the one—ones—you're now holding in your hands.

You may also feel as if I owe an explanation. Why did I do it? Why did I follow the Winter Child? This would be difficult to put into words even if I were a big talker. The closest I can come is to say that the moment I beheld Deirdre, I felt . . . affirmed. For as long as I can remember, my heart has harbored a belief in spite of my logical mind: the belief that the Winter Child truly exists, that she is much more than a character in a bedtime story.

So I ask you, what would you have done? If your most cherished fantasy suddenly had appeared and looked you in the eyes, offered you the chance to become a true part of her tale, would you have refused? Would you have stayed home?

No. I didn't think so.

"Is this some sort of test?" I asked, that first night, as we walked along.

Somewhat to my surprise, once I'd declined Deirdre's invitation to fly through the air, she'd let me set both the pace of our journey and its course. My feet chose the way of their own accord: through the graveyard on the hill outside of town, heading in the direction of the mountains where my father had died. It was almost as if I wanted to say goodbye.

"Is what some sort of test?" she asked in return. This turned out to be a habit of hers. She often answered a question by posing one of her own. Perhaps it simply had become part of her nature. She'd been alone for so long that she'd fallen out of the habit of regular conversation.

"Letting me choose which way to go," I explained.

Deirdre shook her head, and I watched the way the moonlight shimmered over her pale locks. I narrowed my eyes, trying to imagine what she would look like when she was restored to her natural coloring—

midnight hair and dark eyes. I simply couldn't do it. Imagination has never been my strong suit, but it seemed to me that everything about Deirdre fit, just as she was then.

"Of course it's not a test," she answered now. "Why would I want to test you?"

I shrugged, feeling slightly foolish. "I don't know. Because that's the way these things always seem to work, at least in stories. The hero gets tested, needs to prove himself."

She turned her head to look at me then, and I thought I caught a hint of a twinkle in her eye.

"Wait," I said before she could speak. "I don't think I'm a hero. That isn't what I meant at all."

Deirdre bit her lip, as if to hold back a smile. "You might be. You never can tell."

I gave a snort. "I'm a watchmaker, not a swash-buckler, so don't even think about me wielding a sword. I'd probably drop it on my foot and slice off a toe."

"Fortunately for us both"—Deirdre spread her arms wide, the cloak fanning out around her and revealing the dress she wore beneath—"I seem to be fresh out of swords."

"I'm just saying," I plowed on. "I mean, just so you know."

We trudged along in silence for several minutes, both of us looking ahead. What Deirdre was thinking, I couldn't tell. As for me, I was giving serious consid-eration to the physics that allowed me to walk, even though I'd just managed to put both feet in my mouth.

"Does the path we take make a difference?" I asked after a while.

"Yes . . . ," Deirdre said at once.

She tilted her head to look at me, and I caught my breath. *If I live to be a hundred,* I thought, *I'll never get used to those eyes.* They were a color that usually resides only in nature, at the heart of a glacier or in the fine, pale height of a wind-scoured sky. They were beautiful and strange, and they drew me in, right from the start.

What must it be like to possess such eyes? I wondered. *Eyes with the power to see into a human heart?* What did Deirdre's eyes see when they gazed into my heart? Did they see things about it that I could not?

". . . and no," Deirdre went on.

I sighed. "I suppose I should have seen that coming," I remarked.

Deirdre turned her gaze back to the path in front of us, but I thought I caught a glimpse of a smile.

"You know what they say, don't you?" she said.

"I think I do," I answered. "They say that all paths are open to the Winter Child."

"All paths that lead to the living," she amended. "The hearts of the dead are beyond my help."

"But you fly," I protested, then bit my tongue. *It's just like in the old days,* I thought, *when Grace's oma used to tell us stories.* I always had questions, always saw loopholes.

"That was unexpected," Deirdre acknowledged.

"A benefit, if you will, of the brief time I spent in the North Wind's arms. When my time as a Winter Child is finished, my flying days also will be done."

Deirdre cast another sidelong look at me. "To tell you the truth, I don't do it all that often. Like you, I prefer to keep my feet on the ground. That's where the hearts I must heal are to be found. But flying is glorious," she added with a smile. "And I *will* get you to try it sometime, so be forewarned."

"And the path we walk now?" I inquired, bringing the discussion back to where we'd started. I was still curious as to why she'd let me choose our course.

"I thought it might make the transition easier if you chose your own path away from home," Deirdre said simply. "I am accustomed to being a stranger in the world. You are not, and besides . . ."

"Besides what?" I prompted.

"You think you know me," Deirdre answered slowly, as if trying to decide how best to explain. "For you have heard my story all of your life. But every time a story gets told, it changes a little. Things get left out. You don't know me. We've only just met."

"Not a test," I said suddenly, grasping her point at once. "More like an introduction."

Deirdre's face lit up. "An introduction," she echoed. "That's it precisely."

On impulse, I stopped walking and held out my hand. She stared at it, her expression puzzled. Then, without warning, she laughed and placed her hand in mine. It was like holding ice. Never in all my life had I felt anything so cold. It took every ounce of willpower I had not to shiver.

"Pleased to make your acquaintance," I said. "My name is Kai Holmgren. What's yours?"

"Do you know?" Deirdre said suddenly. "I don't think I have a last name, or if I did, I've long since forgotten it." Her mouth gave a funny twist, as if it were full of a taste she couldn't decide if she liked.

"I only have titles, really, don't I?" she went on. "Take your pick. Which shall it be? Princess, Winter Child, or Sorrow?"

"I would like to call you Deirdre, if you'll let me," I answered steadily. "At least it's a proper name."

"Deirdre it shall be, then," said the Winter Child. She took her fingers from mine, and not a moment too soon. My arm was numb up to the elbow. We resumed our walk, continuing in silence for several minutes.

"If that conversation *had* been a test," Deirdre said finally, "you'd have passed with flying colors. You gave both a true and sensible reply."

"Oh, I'm just filled with common sense," I said, surprised at the bitterness of my own tone. "Though if Grace were here, she'd tell you I have too much of it. It made *such* good sense to ask her to marry me. I had it all worked out."

We hadn't talked about Grace, not since we'd left town. But the truth was, even with Deirdre beside me, Grace was always on my mind. For here I was, embarking on precisely the type of journey Grace always had wanted, exploring what lay beyond the horizon. It didn't seem quite fair, somehow.

Still, the fact that I was thinking about Grace irritated me. I had offered her everything I had to give, offered her myself, and she had turned me down.

"And are you sorry?" Deirdre inquired.

"Now I know *that's* a test," I said with a short laugh. "Or at the very least a trick question. How can I know how to answer unless I know what I'm supposed to be sorry for?"

"Sorry for coming with me, of course," she answered. "Sorry for leaving Grace behind."

"No," I said, and as I spoke the word, I felt the certainty of it, right through to the marrow of my bones. "I am not sorry I came with you, and if I'm not sorry for that, then I must not be sorry for the other.

"But I *am* sorry that Grace and I quarreled," I went on, and I felt the truth of this as well. "We almost never do, and we've been friends our whole lives. And I'm sorry that we parted in anger. Our friendship deserved better than that, I think."

"Perhaps there will be the chance to make amends," Deirdre said.

"Perhaps," I said. "I hope so."

Though I noticed that neither of us specified who would be making amends. Was the responsibility Grace's, or was it mine?

We walked all night and on into the morning. Each time we came to a fork in the road, I chose which path to take. The course I set took us higher and higher into the mountains. Deirdre had declined testing me, but it seemed I had some desire to test myself.

I had been happy in my previous existence, working for the watchmaker, figuring out how all the delicate pieces went together and how to mend them if they broke. I'm good with mending broken things, though I never expected to mend a broken heart.

What if I couldn't do it? What if I wasn't strong enough?

"Kai," Deirdre said suddenly, her voice slicing through my troubled thoughts. I felt the cold touch of her hand upon my arm. "Stop."

I did as she instructed, just in time. Two more steps and I'd have walked right off the face of the mountain. In front of us, the path stopped abruptly. The mountains fell away and I could see the world spread out below us. I stood for several minutes, catching my breath.

"The world is a very big place," I observed.

"That is so." Deirdre nodded.

I let my eyes roam over the patchwork landscape. "Have you traveled everywhere?" I asked, and then I winced, for I sounded like a child.

"Not quite everywhere, but close," Deirdre answered.

We stood together, looking out at the great expanse. "I feel very small," I said.

"As do I," Deirdre replied honestly. "But small and insignificant are not the same thing, Kai."

"I think my brain knows that," I said, though my

tone expressed my doubt. "But my heart . . ."

Deirdre laid a hand on my arm. With the other, she pointed across my body to a dark smudge on the horizon.

"Do you see that?" she asked. "That speck of green?"

"Yes," I said. "I think so."

"That is the forest that borders my father's kingdom," she said. "The land of ice and snow, the land where I was born."

I heard the longing in her voice, and suddenly, I saw the way to go. The path we could take to ease the longing in her heart and prove the strength in mine.

Fear, I thought. Hadn't that been Deirdre's mother's innermost flaw? The wound that her shattered mirror had scattered throughout the world. I would not give in to it now.

I reached for Deirdre's hand. Without a word, she reached back.

"Deirdre," I said, "will you teach me how to fly?"

Eleven

Story the Seventh

In Which Grace Sets Out in Search of the Horizon and Discovers More Than She Bargained For

Kai's footprints traveled north. The direction was not surprising.

The Winter Child is taking him home, I thought. *Back to the place where her long journey began. Why?*

I pondered this, and a thousand other questions, late into the night. Common sense suggested I should be getting a good night's sleep so I'd be fresh when I set out the following morning. My brain insisted this was the best course of action. My heart rebelled.

My heart whispered that common sense already had been proved wrong, for common sense had not believed in the Winter Child. It reminded me that Kai and the Winter Child already had a day's head start. Who was to say where they might be by now? Though Oma had told us Deirdre's story for as long as I could remember, I had never heard anyone speak of what might happen to a person who chose to journey beside the Winter Child.

Kai was in her world now. Even more, he had chosen this for himself. Would he cease to age so that he and Deirdre would stay perfectly matched until her task of mending hearts was done?

The trouble with common sense was that my heart had too many questions my mind could not answer. So, in the end, I listened to my heart. Instead of curling up beneath my blankets, I spread out a selection of my belongings on top of them, trying to decide what to pack for my journey. It was not as easy as it sounds. I might have known where I hoped to end up, but I had no idea how to get there. I had no idea how long it would take.

Let's see if common sense can work on this, I thought.

I was going north. That meant cold. But, in spite of the weather at the moment, I knew winter already had given way to spring. It might be cold where I was going to end up, but along the way it would be warm.

I walked to the wardrobe that stood in the far corner of my room. From it, I selected my second-warmest cloak: the green one I often wore for rambling in the woods. I laid it on the bed. Beside it on the floor, I added my sturdiest pair of walking boots, followed by several pairs of socks. The boots might have been heavy, but they would last. And they were well-worn. No blisters, no matter how far I walked. I knew the socks were sturdy and in good repair. Oma and I had knitted them ourselves.

I will need a second dress, I thought, wishing, not for the first time, that I could wear boys' clothes. I chose my third best, one made of sturdy, serviceable calico. It would be a good choice when the weather grew warmer, and it would not take up too much room in my pack in the meantime.

Food to last for several days. A water skin. These, too, were added to my growing pile. I considered for a moment, then added some examples of my needlework. These I might barter for food or sell. Perhaps I could even hire myself out as a seamstress, if necessary. Finally, I placed the shawl I had given Oma in honor of her last birthday on the bed. It was made of pale green silk, embroidered with images of the flowers from our garden. It was too fine to wear, but I could not bear to leave it behind.

I stood back, hands on hips, gazing at my selections.

What else, Grace? What else?

There is nothing else, I realized. Nothing that I could pack, anyhow. My memories of Oma lived inside me, just like my love for Kai. Those would go with me wherever I went.

Go! my heart cried suddenly. *Don't wait for morning. Don't wait another moment to go after who you love. Go now.*

And with that, I was desperate to be gone. Filled with a fierce determination, I bundled the items I had selected into my pack, put on my boots, tossed the cloak around my shoulders, and headed for the door. Here, finally, I paused to look for one last time at the rooms in which I had grown up. On the small table beside Oma's favorite chair was her seed-saving box. I had left it for Herre Johannes.

Oma saved garden seeds every year, each kind in its own slip of paper that was carefully folded so that no seeds could escape. On impulse, I crossed to the box and plucked out a paper containing the seeds of Oma's favorite sunflowers. I carefully tucked it into the bottom of my pack, then slung the pack onto my shoulders. I felt the weight of it settle against my back, felt the way the straps gripped my shoulders. Then I left the apartment, closing the door quietly behind me.

Outside, it was cold. A great round moon, just past full, drifted in the sky. By its light, Kai's footprints were easy to see.

Why? I thought again. *Why?*

I had no answer. But I was not about to let that stop me.

Wish me luck, Oma, I thought.

My breath making fat white clouds in the cold air, I began to walk alongside Kai's tracks.

A girl doesn't need luck, Grace. I suddenly heard Oma's voice inside my mind. *What a girl needs is a good head on her shoulders. She needs to learn to keep her wits about her and her eyes open.*

I will, Oma, I thought. *I promise.*

I reached the end of the street, following Kai's

footprints as they went around the corner. I was so intent on following this strange path that it wasn't until I reached the outskirts of town that I realized the truth:

Kai's steps headed straight toward the horizon.

Twelve

By morning, I was well into the mountains. Though the sunlight made Kai's footsteps more difficult to see, I was glad for it. The mountains, with the entrances to the mines yawning like great dark mouths, were an eerie, unsettling place to be at night. Were it not for the steady pace of Kai's footsteps showing me the way, I'm sure I would have become lost.

Sometime during the night, my ears had caught the voice of a stream, and in the morning light, I could see that my path ran right beside it. It rushed ahead, flush with snowmelt. I continued to walk until I came to a place where the flow of water broadened, becoming wide and shallow.

Here, a clump of fat boulders clustered together, as if inviting weary travelers to sit down and take a rest. I obliged, resisting the temptation to take off my shoes and stockings and wade into the stream.

The thought might have sounded inviting, but it was still early spring and I knew the water would be icy.

I sipped from my water skin, ate a piece of cheese and an apple, and contemplated my surroundings. The mountains were beautiful. They also made me claustrophobic. They pressed close together, leaning in as if wishing to peer over one another's shoulders. I could not see the horizon. I remembered Kai's father, buried to death deep within the earth, and I shivered.

Time to keep moving, Grace, I thought. It was far too early in the journey to be indulging in such morbid thoughts.

I got to my feet, then bent to refill my water skin. I hadn't consumed much, but I had no idea how long my journey might take and I knew I could not be without water. Food I might forage or beg for if it came to that.

The water was cold enough to make me gasp. I filled my skin as quickly as I could, and then returned it to my pack. I settled the straps of the pack over my shoulders and turned back toward the path. I could just see the faint outlines of Kai's footsteps.

I began to walk once more.

By midday the sun had grown warm enough that I could take off my cloak. I added it to the contents of the pack. Without the extra layer of the cloak, the straps of the pack dug into my shoulders. *I will have blisters if this keeps up,* I thought.

In the span of no more than half a dozen steps, I was cross. Cross with myself, but most of all, I was cross with Kai. What did he think he was doing, stealing away in the middle of the night? He hadn't even said good-bye. He had made the most momentous decision of his life without me. He'd gone off and left me behind.

"So much for *me* not loving *you* enough," I muttered aloud as I stomped along.

The path was more uneven now, filled with sharp chips of slippery stone. Somewhere, I felt certain, there had to be a broader way, an easier way; the path the traders with their carts and horses used to cross the mountains.

"But you couldn't go that way, could you? Oh, no," I said, continuing to speak aloud. "You had to go and pick the hard way. You had to follow the Winter Child.

"Ow!"

Busy stomping out my thoughts, I'd let my eyes stray just long enough for my foot to find a large and contrarily shaped stone. It had rolled over, turning my ankle right along with it.

"Oh, fine. You're happy now, aren't you?" I exclaimed aloud, still talking to Kai.

I always had insisted that all you needed to do to get where you were going was to put one foot in front of the other. Kai always had been equally insistent that this only worked if the path was on your side. Apparently, the current path hadn't quite made up its mind as to how it felt about me.

Several steps ahead, a particularly sharp stone sat in the middle of the path. I sent it skittering with a quick, defiant kick.

"All I did was ask for a little more time!" I shouted. "Was that so wrong? We were talking about the rest of our lives. Just because I wasn't ready to settle down right that second. . . . For the record, I never said I didn't love you, Kai. I *do* love you, and if you weren't such a pigheaded idiot, you'd know it!"

At that moment, as if the sound of my voice had startled it into flight, high above my head I heard a bird call, the sound keen and fierce. I paused and looked up, shading my eyes from the glare of the sun. I caught a flash of white as the bird plummeted downward. In the next moment, it spread its wings, the shape of them sharp as an etching against the sun.

It must be a hunting bird of some kind, I thought. *A hawk or a falcon.* City birds I knew well from my many hours on the roof, but I was not as familiar with the wild birds. The bird banked low, and now I could see its dark head. Its body was dappled black and white, like the flanks of a horse.

I watched, my heart in my throat, as the bird's wings beat in the air, soaring upward once more. *He's not hunting,* I thought. *He's simply reveling in flight. Reveling in motion.*

"Oh, how beautiful you are!" I exclaimed, the words rising straight from my heart. "How I wish that I could be like you. How I wish that I could fly!"

What a glorious thing it must be, I thought, *to be able*

to leave the earth behind. To see it spread out below you in all its infinite possibilities.

What did the horizon look like from the sky?

As if it had heard both my words and my thoughts, the bird cried out once more. Then it folded its wings and shot toward the earth. I lost sight of it in a fold of the mountains. As quickly as my elation had come, it abandoned me. I was hot and I was tired.

What do you think you're doing, Grace? I thought. *Kai left without saying good-bye. He left you for the Winter Child. An enchanted princess straight out of a bedtime story. You think you can compete with that?*

You turned Kai away. What makes you think he'll welcome you with open arms? Assuming you actually find him in the first place.

"Stop it. Just stop it," I cried aloud. Thoroughly frustrated with myself, I yanked off my pack and threw it to the ground. "If you're going to think like that, you might as well go home right now. You didn't even last a day. That's pretty pathetic."

I have no idea how the argument I waged with myself would have ended if it had been allowed to run its course. It wasn't. Before I could berate myself any further, I heard the falcon's cry, right behind me. I whirled around. The bird swept toward me, claws outstretched. I cried out and lifted a hand to protect my face.

With a rush of wings, the falcon swept past me. It scooped my pack off the ground and carried it away.

"Come back here!" I shouted. I began to run, stumbling as my feet sought purchase on the slippery stone path. "You can't have that," I yelled. "I need it. It's mine!"

Up ahead, the path took an abrupt turn to the right. I propelled myself around the corner, then skidded to a stop, abruptly confronted by an unexpected confusion of images, a cacophony of sounds. Before I could begin to make sense of any of them, something rough and scratchy was tossed over my head. Sharp pain exploded through my skull. Stars danced before my eyes, and I remembered nothing more.

THIRTEEN

Story the Eighth

In Which Grace Makes a New Friend but Encounters Several Obstacles

When I came to, I was lying flat on my back. A rock the size of a goose egg was digging into my spine. Above my head, the light was beginning to dim; the sun hung low in the sky.

Slowly, I sat up. The motion made my stomach lurch and my head pound. I made a low moan of protest even as I persevered.

"I'm sorry about how hard he hit you," a nearby voice said. I swung my head toward the sound, then wished I hadn't as the world began to spin.

"I wish he hadn't hit me at all," I croaked out. I put my head into my hands until the spinning stopped, then raised it again, more cautiously this time. The figure of a girl about my age swam into view. She was sitting on a boulder near a small, bright campfire, stirring the contents of a pan suspended on a tripod. There was a tent pitched just beyond her.

"Who's *he*?" I asked.

"Harkko, my brother," the girl answered without looking up. "He and Papa think you mean to harm us. They think you're not alone. They've gone scouting to locate the rest of your group."

"They're wasting their time," I said. "I *am* alone."

The girl gave the side of the saucepan a sharp rap with her spoon.

"That's craziness!" she exclaimed. She turned to look at me now, her dark brown eyes wide. Her head was covered by a deep green headscarf. Hair the same color as her eyes peeked out at her temples. She wore a simple dress of coarse homespun wool. Her boots were even sturdier than mine.

"No one goes through the mountains alone." Her eyes suddenly narrowed. "You're lying."

"I'm not lying," I protested at once. "Why would I?"

The girl shrugged. "How should I know? You're a stranger," she replied. As if the fact of my foreignness explained everything and nothing all at once.

"Do you hit every stranger you meet over the head?" I asked.

"It's not a bad plan," the girl answered calmly. "It's always better to strike first and ask questions later. That's the way to stay alive."

"It's also the way to hurt innocent people or make enemies," I observed.

The girl did not reply. She took the pan off the tripod and poured its contents into a mug. Then she brought the mug over to me.

"Drink this," she said. "It will help to ease the pain in your head."

"How do I know it's not poison to put me out of my misery completely?" I asked waspishly.

She grinned. "You don't. But I suggest you drink it anyhow. It really will help you feel better." I accepted the mug, and she sat down beside me. "My name is Petra," she said after a moment, as if making a peace offering.

I took a cautious first sip, grimacing as the hot liquid burned my tongue. The taste was bitter, but not so unpleasant that I couldn't bear it. I took several more sips. Petra was right. After a few moments, my head did begin to feel better.

"I'm Grace," I said, offering my name in return. We sat in silence for several moments.

"Now tell me the truth," Petra said. "How many of you are there?"

"I already told you. I'm alone."

She made a disbelieving sound. "You're a city girl. It's written all over you," she said. "Why would you come on your own into the mountains?"

"I'm following a friend," I said.

"Oh, I see!" Petra exclaimed at once. "You mean a sweetheart."

"No! Well, not exactly," I said. I set the mug on the ground. "It's complicated."

"Sweethearts are always complicated," Petra said. "But if he's jilted you, then it is much more straightforward. He must be caught and punished. Do you have no father or brothers to do this for you?"

"No, I don't," I said. "And Kai didn't jilt me. He . . ."

All of a sudden, I jumped to my feet. Adrenaline surged through my body. "The footprints!" I cried.

Petra got to her feet. "What footprints?" she demanded. "What are you talking about?"

I ignored her. Instead, I dashed from one side of the campground to the other, searching the ground. Kai's footprints were nowhere to be seen.

I had lost the trail. I had no way to follow Kai and the Winter Child.

FOURTEEN

I gave a low moan and sank to my knees, my face in my hands. What was I going to do now? I hadn't even been gone a day, and I had already lost the trail.

"Stop that," Petra said. She gave my shoulders a rough shake. "Stop it right now. That's a disgraceful way to behave! As if you had no courage at all."

"You don't know what I'm up against," I said fiercely, as I raised my head. "You don't know anything about me."

She extended a hand. "Then tell me. Quickly, before Papa and Harkko return."

I took the hand she offered and let her pull me to my feet. Together, we walked over to the fire. Petra gave the contents of a cast-iron pot a stir.

"Now then," she said.

I took a deep breath, and told her.

"I take back what I said about you not having any courage," Petra remarked when my tale was over. "You're either the bravest or the most foolish person I ever laid eyes on. No one can do what you're attempting. No one can follow the Winter Child."

"I was doing a pretty good job of it," I said, "until your brother hit me over the head."

"I'm sorry," Petra said, and I heard the honesty in her voice. "There was no way to know. What will you do now? Will you go back to the city?"

I considered this for a moment. "No," I answered slowly. "I'll continue north, I guess. Surely I'll come to the land of ice and snow, if only I can walk for long enough."

"I wonder," Petra said, her expression thoughtful. Without warning, she stood. She marched over to the tent and disappeared inside it. A moment later, she returned with something slung over one shoulder.

"My pack!" I cried.

"*My* pack, I think you mean," Petra replied calmly.

"You're nothing but a thief!" I cried.

"My people prefer the term 'bandit,'" Petra said in the same infuriatingly calm tone. "It's so much more romantic, don't you think?"

"It amounts to the same thing," I said. "You take what isn't yours."

"But as soon as I've taken it, it *is* mine," she replied. "Be quiet now. That isn't what I want to talk about. I want to talk about how you and I can help each other." She resumed her position beside me.

"I don't understand what you mean," I said sullenly.

"Of course you don't. I haven't explained it *yet.*" Petra opened the pack and rummaged through its contents. After a moment she pulled out my grandmother's shawl.

"Did you steal this?" she asked.

"Of course not!" I replied. "I made it for my grandmother. I did the embroidery myself."

Petra leaned in close, thrusting her face right into mine. "You made these stitches?" she asked fiercely. "You're telling me the truth?"

"I'm telling you the truth," I said. "Now *you* tell *me* why you want to know."

Petra sat back, Oma's shawl in her lap. After a moment she leaned forward and draped it over my shoulder. With one foot, she scooted the pack over until it rested in front of me.

"I've lived in that tent all my life," she said, jerking her head in its direction. "Traveling with my family from place to place, taking what we need to survive. I'm tired of it, so tired I could scream. I want a *real* home. A home with four walls and a bed. I'll never get one as I am now. But if I could do fine work like that . . ."

"You could earn a good living in the city," I said, grasping her point at once. "It's what I used to do. But it didn't happen overnight. It takes time."

"I'm already good with my needle," Petra insisted. "I have to be, don't I? Who else would do the sewing?

I just don't know how to do fancy work like that."

"If I teach you, what will you offer in return?" I asked.

"What you need to know to continue your journey," Petra answered. "I will teach you how to find your way by the light of the stars."

By the time Petra's father and brother had returned to camp, we had settled things between us. I would teach her the embroidery stitches she would need to know to do fancy needlework. She would teach me how to follow the North Star. The first, we would explain to her father. The second, we would keep to ourselves.

"Papa will want to keep you with us," Petra explained as we worked together to prepare the evening meal. "Particularly once I am gone."

"Wait a minute. What do you mean once you're gone?" I exclaimed.

"Shhh," Petra said. "Keep your voice down!"

From across the campground, Petra's brother lifted his head to gaze in our direction. Then he lowered it again, returning his attention to the snare he was mending. The falcon sat on a wooden perch nearby. The falcon's return had been the signal that Petra's father and brother were approaching the camp.

I did not like the look of Petra's brother, Harkko. His face was sullen and brooding, like an overcast sky before a storm. Both Petra's father and brother were harsh-featured. They did not speak much. When they'd first returned to camp, Petra's father had come directly to me.

"You will tell me the truth, if you know what's good for you," he'd said. "You are traveling alone?"

"I am traveling alone," I had said.

He'd given a grunt. "Then you are foolish but not a liar. I could find no other tracks. Make yourself useful and we'll see what I decide."

After that he had gone about his business and had ignored me.

"Tell me what you're talking about," I whispered to Petra now.

She gave the stew a quick stir. "Papa wants to marry me off to old Janos's favorite son," she said in a low voice. "This would give our family the right to trade in the flatlands. We could come down out of the mountains."

You mean you could steal in the flatlands, I thought. "But you don't want to get married," I said aloud.

Petra gave a snort. "Not to old Janos's son. He's a brute. Compared to him, Harkko is a sweetheart. Hand me that plate."

I complied. She began dishing out stew. "I don't suppose it occurred to you to mention this before now."

"It's something else I'm teaching you," Petra answered.

"Oh really, and what would that be?" I asked.

She handed me the stew-filled plate. "How to drive a hard bargain. We'll talk to Papa after dinner," she went on. "He's always in a better mood when his stomach is full. We will tell him this skill you offered to teach me will increase my value as a bride. Say this is how you will earn your keep until we reach the far side of the mountains."

"And what happens then?" I asked, intrigued by her plan in spite of myself.

"That's when you will go your way, and I will go mine. Though that is something we will not mention to Papa, of course."

"No," I said. "Of course not."

After dinner, Petra approached her father and explained what I had offered.

"What good will it do you to know such a thing?" he demanded. He turned his head and spat into the fire. "You will have no time for it. We are not town dwellers."

"But your daughter's marriage will mean you will be able to spend more time in the towns, will it not?" I somehow found the courage to speak up. Petra's father turned his dark eyes on me.

"What is on your mind?" he asked. "Speak up."

"In the course of my work," I said, "I was often called to my patrons' homes. Often they were in the finest parts of town. No one questioned my right to be there. Within reason, I could come and go as I pleased. With this new skill, your daughter would be able to do so, as well."

Petra's father narrowed his eyes and I held my breath. *Now he knows that I see them for who they really are,* I thought. But if I could get Petra's father to believe the skill I could teach her would be an asset . . .

"Perhaps you have more sense than I gave you credit for," Petra's father said at last. "Teach my daughter well."

"I will," I promised.

I had a feeling my life just might depend on it.

Fifteen

I traveled with Petra's family for a week, as we wound our way through the mountains. Though my situation was still precarious, more than once I wondered what I would have done without them. The mountains were much more rugged than I had ever dreamed. No longer having Kai's footsteps to guide me, I might never have found my way across them.

Early each morning and after dinner each night, I showed Petra how to master the elaborate stitches she desired. Once her father and brother had fallen asleep, she taught me about the stars. She showed me how to look for moss on the north side of a tree. Most of all, she provided the bolster my courage needed as I prepared to go on alone, without Kai's footsteps to guide me. In the space of a week, she had gone from being a captor to being a friend.

Nor was Petra the only friend I made during this

time. Though he would go off during the day, when the falcon was in camp, he often stayed close by my side.

"I think he's taken a shine to you," Petra observed on what would be our last evening together. The following morning, our group would come down out of the mountains. Both Petra and I would need to make our escapes that night. Her father and brother had not yet returned to camp. These would be our last few moments alone.

"Perhaps he knows how much I envy him," I said. "I've always wished that I could fly."

"It would certainly make it easier to get where you're going," Petra observed. "Maybe he'll go with you."

I looked at the bird, sitting calmly on his perch. He gazed back at me with clear, gray eyes.

"I always have the sense that he knows what we're saying," I said.

Petra smiled. "Perhaps he does. Falcons are about as smart as birds come. Now," she went on briskly, "tell me again what you're going to do once Papa and Harkko fall asleep."

"I'm going to take my pack and climb that ridge," I replied, nodding at the slope behind us. Petra and I had reasoned that this was the last direction her family would expect me to take. They would assume I would head down, toward the nearest town.

Petra herself would backtrack along the way that we had come. After much discussion, we had decided to leave at the same time. If we staggered our departures and something went wrong, there was a chance whoever went second wouldn't be able to leave at all.

"Now you tell me what you'll do once you reach the city," I said.

"I will ask for the flower vendor, Herre Johannes," Petra recited. "I will tell him you sent me, that you said he might be willing to help. I still don't see why," she added after a moment. "I'll be a total stranger."

She had voiced this concern many times.

"Not everyone believes strangers are not to be trusted," I said. But I could tell that Petra remained unconvinced. On impulse, I went into the tent, opened my pack, and retrieved Oma's shawl. Then I returned to where Petra stood, a puzzled expression on her face.

"Take this," I said as I placed the shawl into her arms. "And give Herre Johannes this message: Tell him I said you wished to put down roots, and that I thought he would be able to help you."

"But you can't—I don't understand," Petra cried.

"You don't have to," I said. "Herre Johannes will know what you mean. And he will know I'm the only one who could have sent such a message. He will know you are a friend, not a stranger.

"Petra," I said. "You have to trust me."

"I know that," she said. "I do. It just doesn't come easily, that's all. And you can't give me the shawl. I know how much it means to you."

"I want you to have it," I said. "All I ask in return is that you tell Herre Johannes I am well."

"I will," Petra promised. She gave me a fierce hug.

"Thank you, Grace. I will never forget your kindness. I hope you find what you are looking for."

"I'm sure I will," I said. "I have the knowledge of the stars to guide me. Now we'd better see about dinner. Everything must seem just like normal."

It seemed that Petra's father and brother would never go to sleep. But at last, all was quiet in the campground. The fire had burned down low, until only the embers glowed in the darkness.

The moon was now a week off of full: no longer a sphere, but a chunky block of white suspended in the sky. This was a mixed blessing. The greater the cover of darkness, the better our chances of escape, yet the less light by which to find our way.

Petra and I waited until we heard her father start to snore before we crept from the tent. In the pale moonlight, I could just make out the two men's sleeping forms. As always, Harkko slept on one side of the fire and Petra's father on the other. With a chill, I realized that Harkko was sleeping on the side closest to the direction in which I would go.

Without a word, Petra flung her arms around me. I hugged her back, squeezing tight. I shouldered my pack. Then, as silently as we could, we each began to make our way out of the campground.

The hair on the back of my neck prickled with each step I took. At any moment I expected to hear the sounds of voices crying out, raising the alarm behind me. I rounded the corner, breathing a little more easily as I did so. Just a few more steps and I would reach the place Petra had showed me, the safest place to begin my climb.

I don't think I'll ever know how it happened—what it was that alerted Petra's father to the fact that we were gone. Perhaps it was simply his own instincts, developed throughout a life spent looking after himself on the open road. No sooner had I reached the place where I would start to climb than I heard an explosion of sounds behind me—voices crying out.

Go, Grace! I thought.

My fingers reached above my head, frantically searching for the handhold Petra had showed me. Sharp pieces of rock rained down onto my upturned face, so loud they sounded like boulders. I heard a second shout, closer this time. *That is Harkko,* I thought.

Finally, my fingers found what they'd been searching for. Digging in with all the strength of my hands, I began to scramble upward. More rocks rained down

"This way!" I heard Harkko's voice shout. I could hear the heavy sound of his footsteps now.

"No," I sobbed.

Then, without warning, the falcon was there. I felt the rush of air as it shot past me, flying up the cliff face. It gave a screech like a war cry. I redoubled my efforts to climb. I felt a second *whoosh* of air as the falcon darted back toward the earth. Below me, I heard Harkko give a terrified cry.

The bird is helping me, I realized. Petra had been right. I had made a second friend after all.

With a final burst of energy, I scrambled up the remaining few feet, then collapsed onto the ledge at the top of the slope. I did not stop to rest, but got to my feet and made my way as quickly as I could along the narrow path at the ledge's far side. Again, I heard Harkko cry out. His voice was answered by the falcon's. Then there was silence.

Keep on going, Grace, I thought. *Don't look back.*

I had walked for perhaps ten minutes when I thought I felt a familiar rush of air. I stopped and extended one arm. The falcon circled around me once, then alighted on my outstretched arm. My shoulder sang at the extra weight, but I kept my arm steady. In the pale moonlight, the bird and I regarded each other.

"Thank you," I said.

The bird cocked its head. Again, I had the eerie sensation that he could understand every word I said.

"I might never have gotten away without you," I went on. "I will never forget what you have done. I swear to you that someday I will find a way to repay your kindness."

The falcon ruffled its feathers, as if in reply. Then, with a force that made me stagger backward, he launched himself back into the sky. I saw his silhouette cut across the moon, then swoop down. Flying on ahead of me, as if to show me the way.

One foot in front of the other, Grace, I thought.

I followed the falcon till the light of the waning moon gave way to morning.

Sixteen

The pattern of our journey now was set. The falcon flew before. I followed behind. The days, which at first held their individual shapes as they were strung together like beads upon a string, at last began to blur and run together like raindrops. I no longer worried about time. Instead, I gave myself up to the journey itself.

It sounds grim, doesn't it? It wasn't. In fact, slowly but surely, I began to realize I was happier than I'd ever been in my life.

Not every day, of course.

There were days when I was lonely. Days when my solitude felt like the weight of a second pack, much heavier than the first. Days when the path beneath my feet seemed full of ruts just waiting to trip me. Days when my feet had blisters, my legs ached, and it seemed as if I was making no progress at all.

It's hard to know if the end is in sight when you don't know how to get where you're going.

On these days, two things kept me on course: my love for Kai and the falcon.

There were the practical considerations of having the falcon as a companion, of course. He was a fierce, determined hunter whose efforts kept me from going hungry. But there was also the simple fact of his presence, the keen edge of his call in the still morning air, the beat of his wings, the sight of his shape silhouetted against the sky. I might not have had a human companion, but as long as the falcon was with me, I was not alone. I was content to put one foot in front of the other.

Finding Kai remained the purpose of my journey, but there were days when I all but forgot about him. These were the days when the journey ceased to be a burden, when I celebrated the fact that each and every step brought me closer to the horizon.

Until the day came when two unexpected things occurred and changed the course of everything: I fell into a river, and my right shoe developed a hole.

It was the second thing that occasioned the first. For many days, I had been walking on the outskirts of a great forest. At times the falcon soared so high above me that he was no more than a dark speck against the sky. At others he swooped down to ride upon my shoulder. For the first time since we had begun our strange journey together, the bird seemed uncertain, unsettled.

"I wish I knew what was troubling you," I finally said, late one afternoon. It was our fourth day skirting the edges of a forest. The line of green seemed to stretch on forever beside me. The trees at the forest's edge were enormous. How large the trees in the forest's center might be, I couldn't imagine.

"Does the forest make it difficult to see which way to go from here?" I asked. "Is that what's bothering you?"

The falcon gave his wings a shake, as if trying to throw off my questions. I felt the sharpness of his claws against the skin of my shoulder. He was always careful never to pierce my skin. My clothing was not so lucky.

"That hurts, you know," I remarked, as I did my best not to wince. "There's no need to take your bad temper out on me."

The falcon butted its head against my cheek. "You are too grumpy," I responded. "I'd help you get over it if I knew what to do. I wish that you could tell me."

Without warning, the falcon launched himself into the air. I stood for a moment, rubbing my sore shoulder with the heel of one hand, watching as the bird arrowed into the sky. Not for the first time, a strange mixture of elation and envy filled my heart as I watched him soar. I resumed walking, my eyes shifting between the ground in front of me and the falcon above as he climbed higher and higher in ever-widening circles.

Then, as abruptly as he'd flown, the falcon folded

his wings and dove back toward the ground. *He has found a way,* I thought. I quickened my pace. I'd gone no more than a dozen steps before my ears were filled with the sound of water. In front of me, the ground rose steeply. I picked up my pace, almost sprinting to the top.

I was standing on a riverbank. The river itself was broad. Its current flowed swiftly into the forest. The falcon sat on a boulder on the opposite bank.

"That's all very well for you," I called out after a moment. "You can fly across. How do you propose I follow?"

I had limited experience with rivers, but even I could tell that this one was much too deep and fast-moving for me to cross. I would have to find another place to try. I put my hands on my hips and surveyed my surroundings.

"I'm going into the forest," I finally announced.

At once the bird sent up a squawk of protest, though he did not move from his place.

"I'm sorry if you don't like it," I replied. "But I really can't see that I have much choice. I don't want to walk along the bank in the opposite direction. That would be turning back. I want to go forward. That means into the forest. Surely you can see that, Mr. Sharp Eyes.

"Why don't you try flying along the course of the river and find a spot where I can cross? Then come back and find me. Please," I finally remembered to add.

At this, the falcon launched himself skyward. He flew across the river and then skimmed above my head, just low enough so that I could feel the brush of his wings against my hair. Flying low and straight, he vanished into the forest.

The sole of my right shoe gave out about half an hour later, which was about five minutes after I'd begun to wonder if I'd made the right choice. Though we'd passed through several woods during the course of our journey, none of them had the feel of this forest. The canopy was so dense that little light filtered down to the forest floor. The air was damp and strangely oppressive. Surrounded by the trees, I lost all sight of the horizon.

I walked along the riverbank. The voice of the river was a great bellow beside me. Beneath the trees even the color of the water seemed subdued, a deep and muddy brown.

All right, so maybe the falcon was right about staying out of the forest, I thought. *Where is he, anyhow?*

At precisely that moment, I put my right foot down on a sharp stone. It pushed its way up through the sole of my boot, which was worn thin by my travels. I gave a yelp of surprise and pain, lifted my foot to extract the stone, and then promptly lost my balance and tumbled down the riverbank to land with a splash in the river.

The water was deep and icy cold. It soaked my skirts in an instant, making it hard to move my legs.

It filled my boots, trying to drag me down. I could feel the swift current, pulling me along with it. I thrashed, desperately trying to keep my head above water.

"Help!" I called out. "Help!"

Through the roaring that filled my ears, I thought I heard a voice return my call. The current swept me around a bend. The river was wider and a little slower here. A broad mudbank extended into the water on the right-hand shore. I swam toward it as best I could. My arms felt heavy with cold.

"Good girl. You can do it," I heard a voice call. I made a final, frantic effort and felt a strong hand reach out to catch hold of my arm. With my other hand, I reached for it with the last of my strength. In the next moment I was on the mudbank, my chest heaving with exertion.

"Gracious, child!" the voice exclaimed. "It's fortunate I happened to come along. Another few minutes in that water, and you'd have been done for.

"Get up now," the voice commanded. "You can't just lie there. You'll catch your death of cold. You come along home with me. I've got a nice fire going. We'll get you warmed up in no time."

Slowly, painfully, I got to my feet. I was so chilled my teeth chattered. My whole body felt bruised and sore. Beside me stood a stout old woman, her face as wrinkled as an apple doll's. She had red cheeks and eyes as bright and dark as a robin's. There was a blue shawl wrapped around her head, a yellow one around her shoulders, and one of purple tied around her waist. She looked like a rainbow come to life.

"There now. I knew you could do it," she said. She placed an arm around my back and guided me up the riverbank. "Come along now. Let's get you home."

Home, I thought. Twice now, the old woman had used that word, and suddenly, a great longing for home rose up inside me. A home with Oma sitting at her sewing, with our flowers blooming all around me. A home with a special place that was mine alone, a place where I might rest.

Tired, I thought. *I am so very tired.*

"There now," the old woman said again, precisely as if she could read my thoughts. We reached the top of the riverbank. "Not much farther now, and you can have everything your little heart desires."

I stopped for a moment to get my bearings and to catch my breath.

I must have been in the river longer than I realized, I thought.

The trees were less dense where I now stood. The forest was more open and welcoming. Bright patches of sunlight slanted down through the trees' branches. In the largest patch of sun sat a cottage. It was painted white and had a thick roof of thatch. A riot of flowers bloomed in front, winding exuberantly along both sides to disappear around the back.

"Oh," I breathed. "A garden. You have a garden."

"Indeed, I do," the old woman replied. "Come along with me. It will feel like yours in no time."

How good it will be to feel the sun on my back! I thought. *How wonderful to smell the scent of flowers!* I wondered if this old woman loved the same kinds that Oma had. Did she have sunflowers?

"My pack!" I suddenly exclaimed. "Where's my pack? I've lost it!"

"Tut," the old woman said. She clapped her hands, and suddenly we were surrounded by a flock of crows.

"This young lady has lost her pack," the old woman said. "Please see if you can find it for her."

The flock of crows flew off at once, their raucous cries loud even over the voice of the river. They wheeled upward, then vanished behind the riverbank. They reappeared almost at once. Each bird held a side of my pack within its beak.

"Be careful, oh please, be careful," I called out.

But it was already too late. With a sound of ripping cloth, the pack disintegrated. My few belongings tumbled through the air. My cloak spread out upon the breeze like a threadbare ghost. The crows began to caw in a great cacophony of sound.

That was when I saw it. The only memento I still had of home. The packet of sunflower seeds from Oma's rooftop garden.

"Oma's seeds!" I cried.

Then, suddenly, the falcon was there, his keen voice cutting across the harsh caws of the crows. Darting among them, as swiftly and accurately as an arrow, the falcon plucked the packet of seeds from the air with his claws.

The crows beset the falcon, shrieking in outrage,

pecking at him with their sharp beaks. The falcon did not let go of his prize. His powerful wings lifted him high into the air, outpacing the wings of the crows. Nevertheless, the black beaks had taken their toll.

The falcon flew straight along the top of the riverbank before turning sharply and disappearing into the forest. The white seed packet was visible in its claws. But so were the black dots spilling to the ground in a fine black rain.

"Oma," I sobbed as the falcon disappeared from view. "Oma."

"That's right, dear," the old woman said. She began to propel me toward the cottage.

"Have no fear. I'll be your Oma from now on. Come into the house and take a rest. Don't you worry about a thing. Granny here can make you forget all your troubles."

Somewhere inside me a voice protested, saying that this wasn't what I'd meant at all. I didn't need a grandmother. I already had one. I didn't want to forget my troubles, for they were a part of what spurred me on. But my head felt fuzzy, my body ached, and the scent of flowers around the cottage suddenly seemed to rise up around me in a great cloud.

"That's right," the old woman coaxed. We reached the front door; she twisted an old brass knob and threw the door open wide. Before me was a room with dried flowers and herbs hanging from its rafters. A cheerful fire burned in a stone fireplace. The scent of something savory cooking in a cast-iron pot wafted toward the door. It was the most peaceful-looking place that I had ever seen.

"You just come right in."

With the old woman's firm hand beneath my elbow for guidance, I stepped across the threshold.

Seventeen

Story the Ninth

In Which Deirdre Receives an Unexpected Welcome

Home!

How shall I describe what it felt like to see it again? What a powerful combination of joy and sorrow!

The great palace of ice and snow in which I had been born rose from the snowfield, solid yet whimsical somehow. The front gate had been made of iron once upon a time, or so my father always told me. But it had long been completely encased in the ice of the surrounding landscape, rendering it as white as the palace behind it. The gates were stuck open, a fact that had always pleased my father. We were a peaceful people. We had no need to bar our doors.

Behind the gates, the palace rose up like a great wedding cake, tier upon tier of floors, of battlements, of towers. In the very center, at the top of the tallest tower of all, was the room my mother had preferred. As I gazed upward, the sunlight caught the windows, casting a sparkle of rainbows across the snow. It was from one of those very windows that I had fallen long ago.

"Look." I suddenly heard Kai's voice beside me. "I think someone is coming out to meet us."

I felt the grip of his hand tighten on mine. All through the hours of our flight, Kai's hand had remained steadily on mine. When at last our feet had touched the earth, he'd swayed a little, like a sailor adjusting to dry land.

We had set down a little ways from the palace. I had wanted to walk toward my home as I once had been required to walk away from it. I tried not to think about the fact that my father would not be waiting there for me. But now, as I watched, a lone figure slowly made its way out of the palace and walked toward the gates.

"I wonder who it is," I said.

"There's an easy way to find out," Kai said with a smile. He took a step forward. I stayed rooted to the spot.

To my dismay and astonishment, my feet, which had carried me through so many foreign lands, abruptly refused to take me any farther. Much as I told myself I wished to, I could not move a muscle. I could not bring myself to take the last few steps, the ones that would truly bring me home.

I'm afraid, I realized. More afraid than I could remember being before.

"I can't," I whispered. "I can't, Kai. It won't be the same. *I'm* not the same."

"Well, of course not," Kai said simply.

I felt a rush of emotion, so foreign that for a moment I could not recognize it. *Gratitude,* I thought. Kai hadn't argued with me, hadn't tried to talk me out of what I felt. He'd simply acknowledged the truth of my words.

I was home. But home was now a place that was both familiar and foreign. *Foreign I can do,* I thought. And suddenly my feet began to move forward of their own free will, for they knew how to walk toward the unknown.

Together, Kai and I walked until we stood directly in front of the open gates. When we got there, the individual who'd come out to greet us bowed low.

"My lady," he said. I gave a start. I'd been so wrapped up in coming home that I'd forgotten the obvious: I was the ruler of this land now. As if to confirm my thoughts, the man before us spoke again.

"Your Majesty, I should say."

"Thank you," I said. *Well, that's going to take some getting used to,* I thought. "I appreciate your welcome. It is most kind."

Oh, for pity's sake, Deirdre, I thought. *Could you sound a little more stuffy?*

Slowly, as if my thanks released him from the need to bow, the man straightened up. Only then did I realize how old he was. For several moments, I gazed into his ancient face. He stared back, his eyes intent on mine. They were dark, and they did not seem to have aged. They were still quick and sharp. I felt my own eyes widen in disbelief.

"You look the same, yet not the same, if you will permit me to say so, Highness," the old man said. "I believe your father would have been proud."

"*Dominic?*" I breathed. "Can it really be you?"

The weathered face broke into a smile.

"I am honored that you recognize me," my father's steward said. "I always told your father that you would, when the time came."

"But how is this possible?" I asked. "I mean surely . . . I've been gone so long . . ."

"Not as long as you might think," Dominic answered. "But no matter. I made your father a promise, many years ago. A promise while he was on his deathbed, though I am sorry to speak of this on your homecoming."

"What did you swear?" I asked, even as I felt my heart cry out. I had known my father would not be here to greet me, had known it before I set out. But hearing his death spoken of was still painful.

"I swore I would be here to greet you upon your return, so that there might be at least one face in your kingdom that was familiar," Dominic answered quietly. "I swore I would do this no matter how long your journey took."

He gestured toward himself. "You see before you the power of this vow."

"I am glad of its strength," I said, speaking from my heart. Then, in a move that surprised us both, I stepped forward and threw my arms around him. I felt Dominic enfold me in a surprisingly strong hug.

"You are like your father," he whispered in my ear. "You inspire love."

"You are the one who knows best about love," I replied as tears blurred my eyes. "For surely your presence demonstrates its power."

I released him and stepped back. "There is someone I would like you to meet," I said. "Dominic, this is Kai."

But as I turned toward him, I saw Kai sway on his feet. For the first time I realized that his teeth were chattering and that his lips were all but blue with cold. I, who am never cold, had forgotten the fact that Kai might be, that he must be, and that he no doubt had been cold for many hours. We had flown through the air on the back of the wind. We stood in the land of ice and snow.

"Quickly," Dominic said. "Let us get him indoors. We will find a way to warm him."

And so, with Dominic supporting Kai on one side and me on the other, we passed through the gates of the palace and I was finally home.

EIGHTEEN

My first weeks in the castle passed in one great blur. There were so many new things to learn, now that I was the ruler of my homeland. I spent many hours each day with Dominic. Kai explored the palace on his own. But when Dominic and I were finished working for the day, Kai often joined us. Much to my delight, the two men liked each other at once. Their talents seemed complementary. Kai was always curious, and Dominic was a natural teacher.

"He is a fine young man," Dominic observed one morning. "He has a good pair of eyes and a keen mind."

We were alone in the room I would always think of as my father's study. I had been going over a list of the mayors in the principal cities of the realm. My interest in names was coming in handy in a way I'd never anticipated. It made it easier to commit the mayors' names to memory.

Dominic and I had had several discussions about the best way for me to meet my subjects, but it was actually Kai who suggested the course of action I decided to adopt. Instead of waiting for people to come to me, I would make a tour of the kingdom. Such a journey would be a good way to show my people that I was as interested in them as they were in me.

The fact that the Winter Child had returned at last to take up her duties as queen of the land of ice and snow had caused great excitement throughout the land. Naturally, my people were curious to see what I looked like. Almost none of them had been alive when I'd first set out on my quest.

I had worried that, having fulfilled the vow he'd made to my father, Dominic's strength would now begin to fade. If anything, it was just the opposite. He seemed to flourish under the responsibility of tutoring me in my new duties. And he genuinely enjoyed the time he spent with Kai.

Kai and I had been given little time alone together since our arrival. This was to be expected, of course, and I was genuinely pleased that Kai had found so much to interest him around the palace and grounds.

As the days went on, however, I found myself lifting my head from my books, as if hoping to hear the sound of his footsteps in the hall. I never did. Instead, I was the one who sought him out. I frequently found him at a window, staring into the distance, lost in his own thoughts.

Though he always turned to me with a smile

when I spoke, there was also always a moment that caused my heart to miss a beat: the moment before he turned, when it was clearest that, though Kai's body was present, his spirit had traveled far away.

"Are you unhappy here, Kai?" I asked one afternoon. Dominic and I were taking a break from our session.

"Unhappy?" Kai echoed. He turned around quickly. "No, of course not. Why do you ask that?"

"It's hard to explain," I said, half wishing I hadn't spoken. What would I do if he said he was miserable and that he wanted to go home?

You know the answer to that, Deirdre, I thought. I would have to let him go. I could not hold Kai here against his will.

"Sometimes you seem pleased to be here, other times you seem far away."

Kai was silent for several moments. "I am far away," he finally said. "Far away from all that is familiar, far from my home."

I pulled in a silent breath. "Do you want to go home?"

Kai shook his head swiftly, and I felt myself relax a little. "No," he said, his tone firm. "I don't. It's just . . ." He turned to look out the window once again. "You have a true place here, Deirdre. I do not."

"Not yet," I said, just as firmly.

"Not yet," Kai said with a slight smile. He continued to gaze out the window, and I wondered if he was thinking of Grace. I moved to stand beside him, our shoulders just touching.

"Give it time, Kai."

"I will." He nodded. He turned to look at me then. "I'm used to being, well, useful, I guess," he went on. "I love exploring the palace, learning how things work, but the truth is, all I'm doing is satisfying my own curiosity. I'm not *doing* anything. I'm not accomplishing anything. It makes me feel unsettled and . . ."

"Useless?" I suggested.

Kai made a face. "I sound like an idiot, don't I?"

"I think you make perfect sense," I said. "In fact, I have a proposition for you. Dominic is going to travel with me, as you know. I need someone to run the palace in our absence. I'd like you to have the job."

"I don't know anything about running a palace," Kai protested.

"But you could learn," I said. "You could figure it out. That's what you're best at, isn't it?" I put a hand on his shoulder. "I want you to be happy here, Kai. I want you to feel that you are needed and that you belong."

"I want that too," Kai said. He lifted a hand and placed it on top of mine. "Deirdre, I—"

"Oh, there you are, Your Highness," Dominic's voice suddenly said from behind us. Kai and I started, then took a step apart. "And good afternoon, Kai," Dominic went on. "I am sorry to interrupt, but I'm afraid it's time for Her Majesty and me to resume our work."

"Kai has just agreed to run the palace in our absence," I said as I turned toward Dominic.

"Excellent," my steward said at once. "That is a

sound choice. I will be happy to answer any questions you have before Her Majesty and I depart."

"Thank you," Kai said, his tone wry. "I'm sure I'll have some."

"See you at dinner," I said.

Kai nodded and moved off down the corridor.

"I apologize," Dominic said quietly as we turned our own steps toward the study. "Perhaps I should not have interrupted."

"No. It's all right," I said.

"Kai is a fine young man," Dominic said, voicing the opinion he'd shared many times before. "But might I ask what plans Your Highness has in store for him?"

"What makes you think I have plans for him?" I asked, unnerved by the question. *Are my feelings so obvious?* I wondered. "He's a human being, not a piece of furniture to be moved from room to room. I'm sure Kai has plans for himself."

"Of course you're quite right," Dominic said at once. We had reached the study. He opened the door, then stepped aside to let me enter first. "I should not have inquired. I have overstepped my bounds."

I waited until we were both inside with the door closed before I replied.

"Of course you should have inquired," I said. "I know my father relied on you to speak your mind. I do too."

"It is my pleasure to assist Your Highness to the best of my ability," Dominic said. He sketched a quick bow.

"Even when I behave like a bad-tempered schoolgirl?"

"Especially then," he said with a smile. We looked at each other for a moment, and I thought I saw both joy and sorrow in his eyes. *Somewhere between the two,* I thought, *is where I want to be, just like everyone else.* I just didn't know how to get there.

"I should help you most when you need it most, Highness," my steward continued. "Would you like me to aid you now?"

"I'm not sure I know what kind of help to ask for," I confessed. "It seems my ability to read hearts is deserting me, just when I need it most."

"I doubt that very much," Dominic replied. "But if I may . . ."

I nodded. "Please, go on."

"I'm not sure you can read a heart in the way I think you mean," Dominic continued. "A way that would let you figure out what that heart will decide ahead of time. No one possesses that gift."

"Then what must I do?"

"Be patient," Dominic answered. "Learn to trust."

"Which one of us?" I asked. Dominic smiled. I caught my breath. I recognized that smile. My father's face had worn it every time I'd solved a difficult puzzle faster than he'd thought I might.

"If you can ask that question, you may need less help than you think you do, Highness," he replied.

"Dominic," I said suddenly. "Will you do something for me?"

"Anything that lies within my power," my steward answered promptly.

"Will you stop calling me 'Majesty' or 'Highness,' at least when we're alone? I'd like you to call me by a proper name."

"What name?" Dominic asked, his tone surprised.

"One that you choose," I replied. "A name that has meaning for you."

"Why do you ask for this?" Dominic inquired.

"Sometimes I feel that all I have are titles," I explained. "Your Highness, Your Majesty, the Winter Child. I know I get to choose my own name when my task is done, but in the meantime . . . I've never really cared for Deirdre," I admitted. "It's just another word for sorrow, after all."

"How do you feel about Beatrice?" Dominic asked.

"Beatrice," I echoed. I held the name in my mouth, felt the way it rolled over and around my tongue. It started out grandly, then seemed to quiet at the end, like a trumpet call rising and then fading in the clear morning air.

"I like it," I said. "Why did you choose it?"

"It was my mother's name," Dominic explained. A shadow passed across his face. "I always hoped I might have a daughter and pass on the name."

"But you didn't," I said, suddenly struck by the fact that Dominic had lived a long, full life and I knew virtually nothing about it.

"No," my steward said with a shake of his head.

"I did not. In fact, I never married at all." He gave a rueful smile as if he had not intended to say so much. "Perhaps I am not the best person to offer advice when it comes to the heart."

"Nonsense," I said at once.

"Thank you," Dominic said softly. He cocked his head, his dark eyes on mine. "The question still remains, though: What are you going to do about Kai?"

"I don't know," I answered, matching his honesty with my own. "I guess I'll just have to wait and see what happens next."

"In other words," Dominic said, "you'll be just like everyone else."

Abruptly, my heart began to pound like a hammer inside my chest.

"*What?*"

"You'll be like everyone else," Dominic said once more. "You may be able to tell whether or not Kai's heart needs mending, but you cannot tell when, or if, it will decide to love. That, you must wait for him to reveal, just like any other girl would.

"Does it please you, to think you might be like everyone else?"

"Do you know," I said, "I think it does. I've never felt like everyone else, not for as long as I can remember. But it might be wonderful to be ordinary."

"Even if it means that, like many others, you end up being unlucky in love?"

"Even if it means that," I said. "Which is not to say

I won't work hard not to be," I added with a smile.

"I wish you luck."

"Thank you." I walked over to the desk and retrieved the paper I had spent the day studying. I handed it to Dominic.

"I will now recite for you the names of all the mayors I am about to meet."

Two days later I rode out from the castle, leaving Kai behind.

Nineteen

Story the Tenth

In Which Grace Makes Several Startling Discoveries

How long did I stay in the old woman's cottage? I cannot tell. Time seemed to pass strangely there, as if the usual rules didn't quite apply.

I was sick for many days, so ill and weak that I could hardly get out of bed, let alone go out of doors. As if all the steps that I had taken had conspired to make me lie down. My dunking in the river simply had been the final straw.

Throughout my illness, here are the things that I recall: the touch of the old woman's hands, the sound of her voice, the never-ending yet always changing scent of flowers. All these things should have been soothing, but somehow they weren't.

No, that's not quite right.

They *were* soothing. That was just the problem: so soothing that I ran the risk of forgetting myself. The old woman cared for me as tenderly as if I had been her granddaughter, and she encouraged me to call her Oma.

Have you ever been a character in one of your own dreams? That's what my days in the cottage in the forest felt like, as if I were on the outside of a window looking in at myself. But all the while, I knew that something wasn't right.

"You're feeling much better, aren't you, Grace?" the woman remarked as she brushed my hair one morning. This was a ritual she performed both morning and night.

Not even my true oma had done this, or at least not since I was a very small child. My true oma hadn't held much store in doing things for me; she'd much preferred teaching me to do things for myself.

"It's no wonder you were all worn out," the old woman continued. "Walking and walking, day after day with no end in sight, not even knowing if you were going in the right direction. How could you, when you didn't know where you were going in the first place?

"Tut."

As she often did when she wished to express disapproval, the old woman made a clucking sound, her tongue hitting against the roof of her mouth. As I'd begun to recover, she'd told me I had rambled during my fever, that I actually had tried to get out of bed, insisting I must keep on walking.

"Falling into that river might be the best thing that ever happened to you." She finished brushing my hair and set the brush on the bed beside me.

"The river brought you to me, and now you can stay right where you are. No need to go tramping through the world. You have me to look after you now."

She stroked her hand along the length of my hair, and then she leaned forward to place her cheek against mine. I wondered what our two faces would look like together, if I could have seen them in a mirror. As far as I could tell, the cottage had none.

"I'll bet you can't even remember what it was you were looking for," the old woman said softly. Her breath felt cool against my cheek. "Or maybe it's *whom*. Whom were you looking for, Grace? Won't you tell me?"

Day after day, she repeated these same questions. Day after day, I kept my lips pressed tightly together, refusing to speak Kai's name aloud.

I won't, I vowed silently.

There was something about the way the old woman posed these questions that alarmed me. The only protection I could give myself was to hold my tongue. Why she should ask these questions, why Kai's name was important, I did not know. I only knew I did not want to answer.

"I can't, Oma," I said, as I did every morning. Doing something of which my own oma would never approve: telling a lie. "I can't remember. I'm sorry."

"Nothing to be sorry for, my dear," the old woman said. "I'm sure you'll tell me in good time." Something about the way she said this always sent a shiver down my spine.

She's right, I thought. Sooner or later, this old woman would learn what she wanted to know. What would happen then, I did not care to guess.

I've got to get out of here, I thought.

As if recognizing it was pointless to ask any more questions this morning, the old woman stood.

"Come along now, Grace. It's time for chores."

"May I work in the garden today, Oma?" I asked as I stood as well. This was also part of the daily routine, my request to go outdoors. But not once since I had crossed the threshold of the cottage had I been permitted to set so much as a toe outside the front door.

"Gracious!" my new oma exclaimed as she snatched the hairbrush up from the bed. "Heavens no. Whatever put an idea like that in your mind? You're nowhere near strong enough to work in the garden. Be a good girl now and make your bed, and then sweep the hearth. I'm going to take this out for the crows. You know how they love it for their nests."

From the hairbrush, she pulled several strands of my hair.

"When I come back, we'll have some hot porridge. That sounds lovely, doesn't it?"

"Yes, Oma."

For the record, I hate porridge and I always have, so that made two lies I told every morning.

The old woman turned and walked to the front door. She plucked a shawl from a row of pegs that hung to one side of the door and wrapped it around her head. Then she opened the door. I took an involuntary step forward. Over her shoulder, I caught a glimpse of blue sky.

This was the moment I hated most of all. The moment she went out and left me all alone, for this was when the walls of the cottage seemed to close in around me. But this morning something unexpected happened. Just as the old woman opened the door, a sudden gust of wind swept into the room, wrenching the door from her grasp and sending it crashing open against the cottage wall.

Cool, clean air, dashed around the room, memorizing its contours. Then it moved to the window at the side of the house, stretching itself out against the windowpane as if to camouflage the fact that it was still inside.

"Gracious!" the old woman exclaimed as she quickly moved to recapture the door. "What a wind there is outside this morning. There must be a storm brewing. All the more reason for you to stay indoors."

She looked at me, her expression severe, as if she expected me to rebel. I remained silent. I remained still. I did not let my eyes stray to the window where I was sure the wind still hovered.

"You remember your chores now, Grace," the old woman instructed. "I don't want to come back and find them incomplete. You know how unhappy it makes me when you disappoint me, don't you?"

"I do, Oma," I replied.

With a final glance around the room, the old woman stepped through the door and closed it behind her. A moment later, I heard the rasp of a key turning in the lock signaling the end of the morning ritual.

She says she loves me, but she makes me a prisoner, I thought. I walked to the window and leaned my forehead against the glass. Sure enough, it seemed that some of the wind still lingered there, pressed against the windowpane. I gulped in one deep lungful of the air and then another.

Help me, I thought. *I've got to get out of here. She doesn't love me, not really.*

What the old woman called love was literally keeping me a prisoner. This love did not think of me, it thought only of itself.

And suddenly, without warning, Kai's face came into my mind. I saw again the way he had looked when he had asked me to marry him. I had feared his love would hold me back, would hold me prisoner. That's what Kai had accused me of when I had turned him down. But now I knew what it was to be held a prisoner by love.

Oh, Kai! I thought. *How I misjudged you, misjudged your love.*

For now that I was thinking clearly, I realized that, like this old woman, I had been selfish. Kai had offered me a gift from his heart. But I had not recognized it, because I had only seen what my heart feared the most.

"I'm sorry," I whispered to the windowpane. "Forgive me, Kai. I think I understand why you chose to follow the Winter Child."

She could do the thing that I could not: look into Kai's heart and recognize the true value of what she saw.

Never again, I vowed. *Never again will I be so blind. Never again will I let fear rule my heart.*

I caught my breath as, in the next moment, the cottage around me seemed to change before my very eyes. No longer did it look homey and snug. Now that my heart and eyes were no longer clouded by fear, I could see the cottage for the ruin it was. The walls leaned inward. The fireplace smoked. Several of the windowpanes were cracked. My heart in my throat, I spun around.

The door sagged on its hinges. It wasn't locked at all! I could not be held a prisoner here, not now that I could see this place for what it really was.

Hurry, hurry, Grace! I thought.

Swiftly, fearing I would hear the old woman return at any moment, I thrust my feet into my boots and laced them up. She had mended the hole in the right one, then had positioned the boots right by my bed, as if in promise of the day I would finally be allowed to go outdoors. But now I knew the truth. The old woman would have kept me a prisoner forever, warping and distorting the name of love. She would have done her best to teach me to believe as she did.

And the moment I finally spoke Kai's name aloud would have been the moment all was lost. There is a power in knowing a name and in speaking that name aloud. A power to summon and a power to banish. But

I had protected Kai. I had kept his name to myself. I had held him in my heart, and my refusal to let him go would help to free me now.

I crossed to the door. It was not quite ajar enough for me to slip through the space. *It's now or never, Grace,* I thought. I put my hands on the ancient wood and eased the door open a little more. The hinges shrieked like souls in pain.

Well, that'll do it, I thought.

Quick as a fish sliding through the narrows, I slipped through the opening. I was almost out when my skirt caught on a stray nail. Almost sobbing now from terror and hope, I yanked it free. The fabric gave way with a high tearing sound. And then I was stumbling down the path, the cackling of crows erupting in the air above me.

"Stop her!" I heard the old woman cry, her voice a wail of fury and despair. "Don't let her leave me alone!"

Straight as arrows the crows dove at me, their sharp beaks aiming for my head. I cried out, raising my arms to shield my face.

Which way? I thought desperately. Which way offered the best chance of escape? For the truth was, I feared both the river and the forest.

And then, suddenly, the falcon appeared. His voice was loud even over the caws of the crows. The bird had not abandoned me. He hurtled downward with talons outstretched, scattering the great black birds, then swept off in the direction of the forest. I followed his flight with my eyes. Through the trees, I caught unexpected flashes of yellow.

I began to run, laughing in joyful understanding, even as the old woman continued to shriek and the crows to caw. The falcon had shown me the way to freedom. It had even sowed the path itself.

All I had to do was follow the row of sunflowers.

Twenty

Story the Eleventh

In Which All the Travelers Who Have Wandered Through This Tale Finally Make Their Way to the Door of the Winter Child

I walked swiftly for the rest of that day, determined to put as much distance between me and the cottage as I could. The falcon flew high overhead, as if to spur me on. After expressing my thanks, I did not speak. I concentrated on making up for lost time. I kept my pace brisk. As the day wore on, the trees began to thin. The air grew colder. Patches of snow dotted the ground.

Late in the afternoon, the forest gave way completely to a broad expanse of white. Here, at last, I paused. For surely this could be no other than the land of ice and snow. Traversing it would be my journey's final phase.

How far is it to the palace? I wondered. I had no food now, no water. I didn't have my warm cloak. I had only my determination not to give up.

Come on, Grace. There's no time like the present, I thought.

Cautiously, I tested the snow with the toe of my

boot. I wanted to be absolutely sure the ground would hold me before I put my full weight down. Snow and ice were nothing new to me, not with the winters where I had grown up. But, as I began to move through this cold, white landscape, it seemed to me that the snow and ice were different somehow. Shaped by the forces that had created the Winter Child. This didn't necessarily make them treacherous, but it did make them unique.

There were no tracks in the snow. Nothing to show that any living thing had ever passed this way before. As far as my eyes could see, there was nothing but a dazzling field of white. I lifted my eyes to where the falcon was circling above me in the sky.

"Which way?" I called out. "Do you know?"

The bird made one last high circle, then arrowed down. He swooped low over my head, and then continued into the path of the setting sun.

"If you say so," I said though, for once, the bird had not given its piercing call. The *whoosh* the falcon's wings made through the air, the crunch of my boots against the snow, the steady rhythm of my heart as it knocked against my ribs, these were the only sounds. It was as if the entire land was holding its breath, waiting for something.

By the time the sun went down and then the moon rose, not even my own exertions were enough to keep me warm. I was tired and hungry. Even the horrible porridge that the old woman had fed me would have been welcome. Worst of all, however, was the feeling that I should be nearing my destination now.

Along about midnight, or so I judged by the position of the moon in the sky, the ground began to incline. I stood for a moment at the bottom of the slope, leaning forward with my hands on my knees, sucking in air.

Come on now, Grace, I thought. *You can't stop now. You'd never forgive yourself. Assuming you don't freeze to death before you get there.*

I straightened, and as I did, I felt the wind come up, frisking around me like a puppy.

"Oh, for heaven's sake!" I exclaimed aloud. "I'm cold enough. If you're going to show up now, the least you can do is to help me."

No sooner did I finish speaking than the wind died away, as if it was thinking things over. Then, having made a decision, it pushed against my back, strong as a pair of hands propelling me upward. I barely had time to snatch up my skirts to keep from tripping over them before the wind pushed me to the top of the rise.

There before me, in a valley curved like a large bowl, stood a palace made of ice, its towers dazzling in the moonlight. A great pair of gates stood open wide, as if to welcome all who approached it. Without warning, I grew dizzy. After weeks on end, after more footsteps than I could number, my destination was now no more than a five-minute walk away.

Then, as I watched, a figure made its way out

through the gates and toward me. Suddenly I was running, no longer caring if I took a misstep, no longer remembering the long miles it had taken to get here, no longer thinking of anything else at all. All I wanted was to reach this solitary figure. To meet him halfway, and more.

"Hello, Grace," Kai said. "It's about time you got here."

Sobbing in relief, I hurled myself into his waiting arms.

TWENTY-ONE

Story the Twelfth

In Which Kai Finds the Key That Opens Many Hearts

"I still can't believe you cried like a girl," I said.

"Well, why not?" Grace demanded. "I am one, aren't I?"

It was the morning following her arrival, and we were sitting in the room I had known she would wish to see most: the palace's tallest tower. The tower from which Deirdre had tumbled as an infant so long ago, thereby setting all our tales in motion.

Grace had slept deeply, which was hardly surprising. She hadn't asked about Deirdre at all, which was. But I knew better than to push her. The last thing I wanted was another quarrel. Once Grace was awake and had eaten a hearty breakfast, I showed her around the palace, finally taking her to the tower. Grace was silent as we climbed the curving stairs. She stood in the open doorway, gazing into the room.

"I wish Oma could have seen this," she said at last.

"I thought that the first time I came here," I answered. "Come and sit by the window. I think you'll like the view. You can see the horizon."

"This may come as something of a shock," Grace said, her tone wry as she followed me into the room. "But I may have seen enough of the horizon, at least for a little while."

"I think it would shock me more if you didn't feel that way," I said.

We settled onto the window seat. In spite of the fact that Grace claimed she'd had enough, I noticed that the first thing she did was look out to see where the ground met the sky. Through the window, I could see a falcon making great lazy circles in the morning air.

"So," I said finally, "here you are. I still can't believe it." In spite of my flippant words at our reunion, I could hardly believe what Grace had done. She had set out after me. She had traveled for countless miles.

"That's several things you can't believe about me," Grace said without taking her eyes from the falcon.

"Well," I answered slowly, "maybe that's because I suddenly feel as if I don't know you as well as I once did."

Grace looked at me then, and I couldn't quite read the expression in her eyes.

"I could say the same about you," she finally replied. "If anyone had told me we'd have such a big fight that you'd go off in the middle of the night without saying good-bye, that you'd leave me to follow the

Winter Child, I'd have told them they were out of their mind. Yet here we are."

"Here we are," I echoed. *And so,* I thought. *What now?*

"I'm sorry," I said, then stared in astonishment. Grace had spoken precisely the same words at the exact same time.

"No, really," I said. "Grace, I—"

"You should let me go first," she interrupted, with just the hint of a smile. "I'm the one who walked for ages to get here, after all."

"I knew you were going to rub that in sooner or later," I said. We hadn't had much time for conversation last night, but we had discussed flying. "You always did want to be first," I went on. "Oma used to say so."

"She did, didn't she?" Grace's smile turned just a little sad around the corners of her mouth. "Perhaps neither of us has changed so very much after all."

A silence fell between us then. Not quite as companionable as those we'd shared in the past, but not so strained as to be uncomfortable, either. It was a waiting-to-see-what-would-happen-next kind of silence. Grace broke it.

"I truly *am* sorry, Kai." Grace spoke quietly. "I'm sorry that we quarreled. And I'm sorry I let you believe I thought that if I married you, your love would require me to change, that it would require me to let go of myself. I'm sorry I believed these things, if only for a moment."

She made a gesture, as if to push away the past. "It was stupid. *I* was stupid. I should have known you better. I *do* know you better. I think"—she sighed—"I think the person I didn't know well enough was myself."

"But now you think you do," I said.

She looked at me, her gaze clear-eyed and steady. "Yes."

"Then that makes two of us," I said. "And for the record, I'm sorry, too. I never should have left without saying good-bye. It seems so childish now, doesn't it? But it felt like the right thing to do at the time."

"So what happens now?" Grace asked. "Do you still want to marry me?"

"If I did, would you say yes?"

"I asked you first," Grace said.

"How about this?" I asked. "I'm going to count to three. When I'm done, we'll each say whether or not we want to get married. We'll answer at the same time, just a simple yes or no. And we'll promise to speak the truth, because, whether we get married or not, we love each other and we always have.

"Will you do this?"

"Yes, I will," Grace said.

She held out a hand. I placed mine into it.

"Ready?"

"Ready."

"One. Two. Three."

"No," we said on the same breath, then stared in astonishment. I'm not sure which of us began to laugh first. We laughed until our sides ached and the tears streamed from our eyes.

"I don't know what's so funny," I managed to say when I could take a breath. "I walked out on you, you walked half the world to find me, and we don't want to be together. Oma would never have approved of this. Didn't she say stories were always supposed to end in happily ever after?"

"Who's to say ours won't still do that?" Grace asked. "I don't know about you, but I'm laughing in relief. I was so afraid I'd walked all this way only for us to hurt each other again."

"Why did you come after me?" I asked.

Grace was silent for a moment, her fingers fiddling with a tassel on the window-seat cushion.

"Because I had to," she finally said. "I couldn't bear the thought that you'd gone away in anger, though when I discovered that you'd left, I got pretty mad myself. And also . . ." Her voice trailed off. "I was afraid."

"Afraid," I echoed.

"Afraid that I'd never see you again," Grace said, her tone implying I was being stupid. Her fingers continued to worry the tassel. "What's she like?"

"What's who like?"

Grace heaved the cushion at my head. "Don't be an idiot. The Winter Child, of course."

"She's difficult to describe," I said. "She's very beautiful, of course."

"Oh, of course," Grace said.

I picked up the cushion and threw it back at her. "But in all my life, I don't think I've ever seen anyone so sad. You and I—we've always had each other, even when we've made mistakes. The fact that you came after me proves that. But Deirdre's spent years and years with no one at all."

"Except that now she has you," Grace said.

I made a face. "Is it that obvious? Being that obvious is just pathetic."

Grace gave a quick laugh. "You've never been pathetic, Kai," she said. "And the only reason I know you love her is because I know you so well."

She sat up a little straighter then, as if I'd poked her with a pin. "Do you mean to say you haven't told her?"

"Of course I haven't told her," I said. "How can I? She's a queen and what am I? A watchmaker's apprentice. Besides, I had pretty much given her the impression I wanted to marry you."

"Well, no wonder you were so happy to see me show up," Grace said with a laugh.

"That's it. I take it all back. I never missed you for a minute."

"Oh, yes you did," Grace protested.

"Yes, I did," I said more seriously. "I worried about you, too."

"Did you know I would come after you?" Grace asked.

"I didn't exactly *know* it," I answered slowly. "It was more a feeling that I had, as if I could sense your determination to find me, no matter what. It's part of why I agreed to stay behind while Deirdre toured the country."

"When will she be back?"

"She's expected today," I said.

"And then you'll tell her that you love her," Grace said.

I stood up. "It's not that simple, Grace," I protested.

She got up in turn, moving to grasp me by the shoulders.

"Yes it is, Kai," she said. "In its heart, in *your* heart, love is very simple. That is part of its great strength. It's only the world's expectations that complicate things."

"That's precisely my point," I said.

"Which means," Grace continued, her voice rising to carry over mine, "that you should tell Deirdre how you feel about her without delay. The worst that can happen is that she doesn't feel the same as you do, right?"

"Well, *yes*," I said tartly.

"But that would be no worse than the situation you're in right now," Grace said. "Not knowing how she really feels. Being afraid to speak up."

"I'm not afraid," I protested.

"Then prove it, Kai," Grace said. "If you don't tell her, you'll always wonder what might have happened. Surely you don't want to live a life of regret."

Grace made good sense, I had to admit. "What makes you so smart all of a sudden?" I asked.

Grace gave me a fierce hug. "I've had a lot of time

to think things over," she said. She released me and stepped back. Then, to my surprise, she raised a hand to my cheek, just as her grandmother always had.

"You have such good eyes, Kai," Grace said softly. "Don't waste what they can see."

"I won't," I promised.

In the next moment, I heard the falcon's piercing cry. Grace moved back to the window, undid the latch, and opened the casement. With a great rush of wings, the bird swept inside. It made a circuit of the room, then darted out again. Grace leaned out, the better to see the bird in flight.

"There's a train of horses coming," she said. "I think the Winter Child is back."

TWENTY-TWO

Story the Thirteenth

In Which Many Important Words Are Spoken

On my second homecoming, Kai waited for me at the palace gates with Grace at his side. They stood close together, hands clasped, and I felt my heart begin to sing with joy and weep with sorrow all at the same time.

I came so close, I thought. *So close to finding love.* But it seemed it was not to be.

"Welcome home," Kai said, and then he smiled. "I'd like to introduce you to my oldest friend, Grace Andersen. She has traveled many miles to find me."

"Welcome, Grace," I said. *How right they look together,* I thought. *How long will it be before Kai leaves, I wonder?*

"Thank you, Your Highness," Grace said formally. She let go of Kai's hand to execute a curtsy. Then she stood quietly, hands at her sides.

"How did Deirdre do with the list of names?" Kai inquired of Dominic as the household servants rushed forward to help the two of us dismount. As my feet hit the snow, I gave a quick shiver. Why had I never noticed the way the cold seeped up through the soles of my shoes?

"She knew every name by heart. Not that I expected anything less, of course," Dominic replied. "And now, Your Highness"—he bowed low—"with your permission, I will retire indoors. My tired old bones are cold and would be happy for a little rest."

"It is cold today, isn't it?" I replied.

Dominic straightened up with a snap.

"What did you say?" he barked.

"I said I thought that it was cold today," I answered. "In fact, I can't remember when . . ." As the enormity of what I was saying hit me, my voice trailed off.

"What? What is it?" I heard Kai ask.

"I'm cold," I whispered. "Oh, Kai, I'm cold."

"It's happened at last," Dominic said, and I could hear the awe and wonder in his voice. "The last heart, her own, has been made whole. She is herself again, a Winter Child no longer."

At this, a great cheer went up. The servants who had gathered to welcome us fell to their knees as if with one body.

"Please," I said through teeth that suddenly wanted very badly to chatter. "Please rise. If I'm cold, I'm sure you are too. Let us all go inside."

But as I went to walk, I swayed on my feet, as if my body was suddenly a foreigner to itself. At once, Kai was at my side. He took off his cloak and draped it around my shoulders. It was warm from his body. He placed one arm around my back. With one hand, he grasped my elbow, firmly.

"Let us go in," he said.

And so I entered the palace of ice with Kai's arm around me.

A short time later we were seated in the tower room, Kai, Grace, and I. Dominic had retired to his rooms. I had changed from my traveling clothes to a gown of pale blue silk, with a dark blue shawl around my shoulders. I was still having trouble adjusting to the cold.

Before I'd joined Kai and Grace, I'd stood in front of the mirror in my room, studying my reflection for several moments. My face looked much as it always had. But my hair and eyes were both growing darker. All save a streak of white hair beginning at my left temple, a permanent reminder of my years as a Winter Child. I lifted a hand to touch it.

I'm glad it's there, I thought. *I spent too much time as a Winter Child for that part of me to ever be forgotten.*

I made my way to the tower. Even from this secluded location, I could feel a buzz of excitement throughout the palace. First the Winter Child had returned home, and now she was a Winter Child no longer.

I wish I could tell you that I shared their excitement. The truth is, for the first time in a long time, I was absolutely terrified.

As I entered the room, I looked across it to Kai. He was sitting in a great wooden chair. Since ushering me into the castle, he had kept his distance. His face was tight, an expression that said he was dreading either the speaking or the hearing of bad news.

Grace sat on the window seat. At my insistence, she'd selected several dresses from my wardrobe. The one she was wearing now was a rich and vibrant green. A peregrine falcon perched on the windowsill beside her.

Just as we'd entered the palace gates, the bird had swooped down to land upon her shoulder. Grace had accepted his presence as if they were old companions, and so the two had come indoors together. She reached up absently from time to time to stroke a finger along the bird's white throat.

The room was filled with silence. A silence that was mine to break. *Quit stalling, Deirdre,* I thought.

"I suppose you'd like an explanation," I said.

"Only if you want to give one," Kai spoke up quickly.

I heard Grace make an exasperated sound. "Of course she wants to give one," she said. "Just as we both want to hear it."

She looked at me then, our eyes meeting for the first time. In hers I saw a strange mixture of amusement, irritation, and compassion.

"You'll have to forgive him," she said. "He's feeling a little confused at the moment."

"I know just how he feels," I replied.

Grace cocked her head then, in perfect imitation of the bird beside her. "I didn't think I'd like you," she said suddenly. "And I was *very* sure I didn't want to."

"I could say the same about you," I said, and with that, I discovered that we were grinning like fools. In the next moment, as much to her surprise as to mine, Grace rose to her feet and curtsied low before me.

"Then may I ask you to speak, Your Highness?" she asked. "Will you explain why you are no longer a Winter Child?"

"I will," I answered, a good deal more calmly and regally than I felt.

Grace resumed her position on the window seat.

"I do not need to tell you how I became a Winter Child," I said. "For that tale is well-known. Just as it is known that, of all the hearts I would be called upon to mend, the one that would always remain out of reach would be my own.

"Only one thing could mend my heart. Only one thing could make it whole: the heart that was my heart's true match."

I heard Kai catch his breath.

So quick, he is so quick, I thought. He looked at me then, and I met his gaze. It took everything I had to keep mine steady.

"It wasn't my heart you needed at all, was it?" he said quietly.

"I wouldn't say that," I answered. "I *do* need your heart, Kai."

"What? Wait a minute." Grace suddenly exploded. "What are you two talking about?"

Kai turned to look at her. "Can't you guess?" he asked. "We're talking about you, of course."

"It was your heart that I needed, Grace," I said. "A heart willing to set out upon a journey of its own free will, a journey with no signposts along the way and no foreseeable end in sight. A journey that could only be completed by always putting one foot in front of the other.

"It is the heart willing and able to do all this that is the true match to mine. For this is precisely what my own heart was called upon to do."

"But I thought," Grace said, and then she paused. She shook her head, as if hoping to rearrange her thoughts. "I thought you loved Kai. What about his heart?"

"I do love Kai," I said, though I was finding it hard to speak around the lump in my throat. "I love him even though we must part. I need his heart. But his heart was not designed to mend mine. Yours was."

"Are you going to send me away?" Kai asked. I turned and saw that he had risen to his feet. "Is that what you want?"

"Of course it isn't what I want," I said.

"Then *why*?" Kai cried.

"Because—" I broke off. "Wait a minute," I said. "What do you mean, why? Don't you know?"

"Oh, for heaven's sake, Kai!" Grace exclaimed. "Don't just stand there. Tell her!"

"I'm trying to," Kai snapped back. "But you keep interrupting."

"Tell me what?" I asked.

"I love you," Kai said quietly. But in his quiet tone, I heard absolute certainty.

A great wave of emotion rolled through me.

"I think I have to sit down."

Kai laughed then, and the whole room suddenly was flooded with bright sunlight. From the windowsill, the falcon gave a sweet, sharp cry.

"But I thought you loved Grace," I said.

"And so I do," Kai replied. "But not the way that I love you." He knelt before me and took my hands. "The truth is, I've loved you my whole life." He stood and gently drew me to my feet. "Close your eyes, Grace," he said over his shoulder.

I was laughing as my true love placed his lips on mine. Kai's lips were warm. By the time the kiss was over, I knew I would never be cold again. With Kai's arm still around me, I turned to Grace. She was standing by the window with the sun on her face and the falcon by her side. Her eyes were wide open. In them I thought I caught the glint of tears.

"Kai will tell you I almost never do what he says."

"Thank you," I said. "For your heart has helped to mend mine twice. I would like it very much if there was something I could do for yours."

"But you're no longer the Winter Child," Grace protested.

"True enough," I answered. "Nevertheless, it lies

within my power to grant a wish to the heart that has restored my own. What would your heart choose, Grace, if it could?"

"The same as it has always chosen," Grace replied. "My heart has never wanted to be in just one place. It has always longed for the journey, to see what lies over the horizon.

"It isn't that I don't love familiar things. It's that I love the unknown more."

At her words, the falcon suddenly spread its wings. It threw back its head and made the tower room echo with its cry. Without warning, the sunlight became blinding. I heard both Grace and Kai cry out, even as I lifted a hand to shield my eyes.

When I lowered it, the falcon was gone. In its place stood a tall young man with fine, pale skin and wide gray eyes. Long dark hair brushed the tops of his shoulders.

"Oh dear," Grace said.

The young man threw back his head and laughed, a bright, pure sound. Then he knelt at Grace's feet. He extended a hand, palm up. After a moment's hesitation, Grace placed one of hers within it.

"Thank you," the young man said simply. "Your words have rescued me from an enchantment I have carried for many years."

"Now I'm the one who wants to sit down," Grace said.

The young man chuckled. Still holding Grace's hand in his, he rose to his feet, then turned to me with a bow.

"Your Majesty," he said. "I hope you will forgive my somewhat unusual arrival."

"Gladly," I said, my tone warm with surprise. "On the condition that you explain yourself."

"Long ago," the young man said, "I made a great mistake: I mistook false love for true. The young woman I rejected was a powerful sorceress. She placed a curse and a burden upon me, dooming me to wear the form of a falcon until I could find a heart that would choose me of its own free will, yet not be aware that it had done so."

"A heart that would choose the unknown," Kai suddenly said.

The young man nodded. "Precisely. I have flown throughout the world for many years, so many that I began to despair of ever breaking the curse."

He turned back to Grace.

"Until one day, I saw a girl in the mountains. A girl who refused to give up, who kept her wits about her. My heart has been yours from that day to this one."

"I don't suppose your name is Peregrine, is it?" Grace asked.

"It's Constantin, as a matter of fact," the young man said.

"Constantin," Grace echoed. "And will you be as true as your name?"

"With all my heart."

"In that case," Grace said, her tone mischievous, "I will give you mine again, knowingly this time. I only wish I could have learned how to fly."

"I will grant that wish, if you'll let me," I said.

"If you will, for three weeks out of every month, you will both be as you are now. But in the fourth week, Constantin may return to the form of a bird and, since Grace's heart has chosen his, hers may also. Let your body soar as your heart has always longed to, and let this be the final gift of the Winter Child."

"I thank you with all my heart," Grace said.

"As I thank you for the gift of mine."

Epilogue

A Few Thoughts Concerning Happy Endings

And so it came to pass that the two couples were married in a single ceremony in the great palace of ice. People came to celebrate from miles around.

Grace sent word to the city far away. Petra and Herre Johannes came to the wedding, traveling all the way in Herre Johannes's flower wagon. He presented Deirdre with a bunch of snow drops, which she carried as a wedding bouquet. Petra gave Grace back her oma's shawl.

The wedding feast lasted for a full week, after which Petra and Herre Johannes began their journey home, while Grace and Constantin took to the skies. But Grace and Constantin promised to return to the land of ice and snow each year, for the bonds of love and friendship between the two couples were strong.

Of course they all lived happily ever after, and not just because that is the way these things usually go, but because their hearts had been tested and had remained true. That is the happiest ending of all.

"Well?" Kai asked, just at sunset on the day the wedding festivities concluded. He and his bride stood together at the palace gates, watching Grace and Constantin disappear from view.

"Have you decided?"

"I have." His new wife nodded. She leaned back against him, and then tilted her face to look into his. "I wonder if you can guess what my new name will be."

"I can tell you what I always thought it should be," Kai said. "Will that do just as well?"

She turned in his arms then, so that they were face-to-face. "Tell me."

"Hope," said Kai.

At the sounding of this single syllable, she threw her arms around him.

"I love you, Kai."

"I take it I got it right, then," Kai said.

She thumped a fist against his chest. "There's no need to be insufferable."

And now, finally, Deirdre, the Winter Child, she who had once been named for sorrow, chose a new name, and the name that she chose was Hope. For, now that she was restored to her true self at last, she understood that this was the name her heart had carried within it all along.

For even as the winter carries within it the seeds of spring, her heart had nourished, as all hearts must, the strong yet fragile seeds of hope.

Author's Note

The structure of *Winter's Child* is a little different from other stories I've created for the Once upon a Time series. This is a direct inspiration from my source material, Hans Christian Andersen's "The Snow Queen." As a matter of fact, the official title is "The Snow Queen: A Tale in Seven Stories." As is the case with *Winter's Child*, in Andersen's tale each individual "story" has its own heading giving a hint of what's to come.

In the original, the queen herself is pretty much the bad guy. As I am never that interested in stories where one character is always good and another always bad, I decided to mix things up. It also took me more than seven stories to get my characters where I wanted them to go! I tell myself this is okay as my tale is much longer. I hope you enjoy the *Winter's Child* journey. May it inspire your heart on the journeys it will make.

DON'T MISS THIS MAGICAL TITLE
IN THE ONCE UPON A TIME SERIES!

Belle

CAMERON DOKEY

Celeste. April. Belle.

Everything about my sisters and me was arranged in this fashion, in fact. It was the way our beds were lined up in our bedroom; our places at the dining table, where we all sat in a row along one side. It was the order in which we got dressed each morning and had our hair brushed for one hundred and one strokes each night. The order in which we entered a room or left it, and were introduced to guests. The only exception was when we were allowed to open our presents all together, in a great frenzy of paper and ribbons, on Christmas morning.

This may seem very odd to you, and you may wonder why it didn't to any of us. All that I can say is that order in general, but most especially the order in which one was born, was considered very important in the place where I grew up. The oldest son inherited his father's house and lands. Younger daughters did not marry unless the oldest had first walked down the aisle. So if our household paid strict attention to which sister came first, second, and (at long last) third, the truth is that none of us thought anything about the arrangement at all.

Until the day Monsieur LeGrand came to call.

Monsieur LeGrand was my father's oldest and closest friend, though Papa had seen him only once and that when he was five years old. In his own youth, Monsieur LeGrand had been the boyhood friend of Papa's father, Grand-père Georges. It was Monsieur LeGrand who had brought to Grand-mère Annabelle the sad news that her young husband had been snatched off the deck of his ship by a wave that curled around him like a giant fist, then picked him up and carried him down to the bottom of the ocean.

In some other story, Monsieur LeGrand might have stuck around, consoled the young widow in her grief, then married her after a suitable period of time. But that story is not this one. Instead, soon after reporting his sad news, Monsieur LeGrand returned to the sea, determined to put as much water as he could between himself and his boyhood home.

Eventually, Monsieur LeGrand became a merchant specializing in silk, and settled in a land where silkworms flourished, a place so removed from where he'd started out that if you marked each city with a finger on a globe, you'd need both hands. Yet even from this great distance, Monsieur LeGrand did not forget his childhood friend's young son.

When Papa was old enough, Grand-mère Annabelle took him by the hand and marched him down to the waterfront offices of the LeGrand Shipping Company. For, though he no longer lived in the place where he'd grown up, Monsieur LeGrand maintained a presence in our seaport town. My father then began the process that took him from being the boy who swept the floors and filled the coal scuttles to the man who knew as much about the safe passage of sailors and cargo as anyone.

When that day arrived, Monsieur LeGrand made Papa his partner, and the sign above the waterfront office door was changed to read LEGRAND, DELAURIER AND COMPANY. But nothing Papa ever did, not marrying Maman nor helping to bring three lovely daughers into the world, could entice Monsieur LeGrand back to where he'd started.

Over the years, he had become something of a legend in our house. The tales my sisters and I spun of his adventures were as good as any bedtime stories our nursemaids ever told. We pestered our father with endless questions to which he had no answers. All that he remembered was that Monsieur LeGrand had been straight and tall. This was not very satisfying, as I'm sure you can imagine, for any grown-up might have looked that way to a five-year-old.

Then one day—on my tenth birthday, to be precise—a letter arrived. A letter that caused my father to return home from the office in the middle of the day, a thing he never does. I was the first to spot Papa, for I had been careful to position myself near the biggest of our living room windows, the better to watch for any presents that might arrive.

At first, the sight of Papa alarmed me. His face was flushed, as if he'd run all the way from the waterfront. He burst through the door, calling for my mother, then dashed into the living room and caught me up in his arms. He twirled me in so great a circle that my legs flew out straight and nearly knocked Maman's favorite vase to the floor.

He'd had a letter, Papa explained when my feet were firmly on the ground. One that was better than any birthday present he could have planned. It came from far away, from the land where the silkworms flourished, and it informed us all that, at long last, Monsieur LeGrand was coming home.

Not surprisingly, this threw our household into an uproar. For it went without saying that ours would be the first house Monsieur LeGrand would come to visit. It also went without saying that everything needed to be perfect for his arrival.

The work began as soon as my birthday celebrations were complete. Maman hired a small army of extra servants, as those who usually cared for our house were not great enough in number. They swept the floors, then polished them until they gleamed like gems. They hauled the carpets out of doors and beat them. Every single picture in the house was taken down from its place on the walls and inspected for even the most minute particle of dust. While all this was going on, the walls themselves were given a new coat of whitewash.

But the house wasn't the only thing that got polished. The inhabitants got a new shine as well. Maman was all for us being reoutfitted from head to foot, but here, Papa put his foot down. We must not be extravagant, he said. It would give the wrong impression to Monsieur LeGrand. Instead, we must provide his mentor and our benefactor with a warm welcome that also showed good sense, by which my father meant a sense of proportion.

So, in the end, it was only Papa and Maman who had new outfits from head to foot. My sisters and I each received one new garment. Celeste, being the oldest, had a new dress. April had a new silk shawl. As for me, I was the proud owner of a new pair of shoes.

It was the shoes that started all the trouble, you could say. Or, to be more precise, the buckles.

They were made of silver, polished as bright as mirrors. They were gorgeous and I loved them. Unfortunately, the buckles caused the shoes to pinch my feet, which in turn made taking anything more than a few steps absolute torture. Maman had tried to warn me in the shoe shop that this would be the case, but I had refused to listen and insisted the shoes be purchased anyhow.

"She should never have let you have your own way in the first place," Celeste pronounced on the morning we expected Monsieur LeGrand.

My sisters and I were in our bedroom, watching and listening for the carriage that would herald Monsieur LeGrand's arrival. Celeste was standing beside her dressing table, unwilling to sit lest she wrinkle her new dress. April was kneeling on a cushion near the window, the silk shawl draped around her shoulders, her own skirts carefully spread out around her. I was the only one actually sitting down. Given the choice between the possibility of wrinkles or the guarantee of sore feet, I had decided to take my chances with the wrinkles.

But though I was seated, I was hardly sitting still. Instead, I turned my favorite birthday present and gift from Papa—a small knife for wood carving that was cunningly crafted so that the blade folded into the handle—over and over between my hands, as if the action might help to calm me.

Maman disapproves of my wood carving. She says it isn't ladylike and is dangerous. I have pointed out that I'm just as likely to stab myself with an embroidery needle as I am to cut myself with a wood knife. My mother remains unconvinced, but Papa is delighted that I inherited his talent for woodwork.

"And put that knife away," Celeste went on. "Do you mean to frighten Monsieur LeGrand?"

"Celeste," April said, without taking her eyes from the street scene below. "Not today. Stop it."

Thinking back on it now, I see that Celeste was feeling just as nervous and excited as I was. But Celeste almost never handles things the way I do, or April either, for that matter. She always goes at things head-on. I think it's because she's always first. It gives her a different view of the world, a different set of boundaries.

"Stop what?" Celeste asked now, opening her eyes innocently wide. "I'm just saying Maman hates Belle's knives, that's all. If she shows up with one today, Maman will have an absolute fit."

"I know better than to take my wood-carving knife into the parlor to meet a guest," I said as I set it down beside me on my dressing table.

"Well, yes, you may *know* better, but you don't always *think*, do you?" Celeste came right back. She swayed a little, making her new skirts whisper to the petticoats beneath as they moved from side to side. Celeste's new dress was a pale blue, almost an exact match for her eyes. She'd wanted it every bit as much as I'd wanted my new shoes.

"For instance, if you'd thought about how your feet might *feel* instead of how they'd *look*, you'd have saved yourself a lot of pain, and us the trouble of listening to you whine."

I opened my mouth to deny it, then changed my

mind. Instead, I gave Celeste my very best smile. One that showed as many of my even, white teeth as I could. I have very nice teeth. Even Maman says so.

I gave the bed beside me a pat. "If you're so unconcerned about the way you look," I said sweetly, "why don't you come over here and sit down?"

Celeste's cheeks flushed. "Maybe I don't want to," she answered.

"And maybe you're a phony," I replied. "You care just as much about how you look as I do, Celeste. It just doesn't suit you to admit it, that's all."

"If you're calling me a liar—," Celeste began hotly.

"Be quiet!" April interrupted. "I think the carriage is arriving!"

Quick as lightning, Celeste darted to the window, her skirts billowing out behind her. I got to my feet, doing my best to ignore how much they hurt, and followed. Sure enough, in the street below, the grandest carriage I had ever seen was pulling up before our door.

"Oh, I can't see his face!" Celeste cried in frustration, as we saw a gentleman alight. A moment later, the peal of the front doorbell echoed throughout the house. April got to her feet, smoothing out her skirts as she did so. In the pit of my stomach, I felt a group of butterflies suddenly take flight.

I really *did* care about the way I looked, if for no other reason than how I looked and behaved would reflect upon Papa and Maman. All of us wanted to make a good impression on Monsieur LeGrand.

"My dress isn't too wrinkled, is it?" I asked anxiously, and felt the butterflies settle down a little when it was Celeste who answered.

"You look just fine."

"The young ladies' presence is requested in the parlor," our housekeeper, Marie Louise, announced from the bedroom door. Marie Louise's back is always as straight as a ruler, and her skirts are impeccably starched. She cast a critical eye over the three of us, then gave a satisfied nod.

"What does Monsieur LeGrand look like, Marie Louise?" I asked. "Did you see him? Tell us!"

Marie Louise gave a sniff to show she disapproved of such questions, though her eyes were not unkind.

"Of course I saw him," she answered, "for who was it who answered the door? But I don't have time to stand around gossiping any more than you have time to stand around and listen. Get along with you, now. Your parents and Monsieur LeGrand are waiting for you in the parlor."

With a rustle of skirts, she left.

My sisters and I looked at one another for a moment, as if catching our collective breath.

"Come on," Celeste said. And, just like that, she was off. April followed hard on her heels.

"Celeste," I begged, my feet screaming in agony as I tried to keep up. "Don't go so fast. Slow down."

But I was talking to the open air, for my sisters were already gone. By the time I made it to the bedroom door, they were at the top of the stairs. And by the time I made it to the top of the stairs, they were at the bottom. Celeste streaked across the entryway, then paused before the parlor door, just long enough to give her curls a brisk shake and clasp her hands in front of her as was proper. Then, without a backward glance, she marched straight into the parlor with April trailing along behind her.

Slowly, I descended the stairs, then came to a miserable stop in the downstairs hall.

Should I go forward, I wondered, *or should I stay right where I am?*

No matter who got taken to task over our entry later—and someone most certainly would be—there could be no denying that I was the one who would look bad at present. I was the one who was late. I'd probably already embarrassed my parents and insulted our honored guest. *Perhaps I should simply slink away, back to my room,* I thought. I could claim I'd suddenly become ill between the top of the stairs and the bottom, that it was in everyone's best interest that I hadn't made an appearance, particularly Monsieur LeGrand's.

And perhaps I could flap my arms and fly to the moon.

That's when I heard the voices drifting out of the parlor.

There was Maman's, high and piping like a flute. Papa's with its quiet ebb and flow that always reminds me of the sea. Celeste and April I could not hear at all, of course. They were children and would not speak unless spoken to first. And then I heard a voice like the great rumble of distant thunder say:

"But where is la petite Belle?"

And, just as real thunder will sometimes inspire my feet to carry me from my own room into my parents', so too the sound of what could be no other than Monsieur LeGrand's voice carried me through the parlor door and into the room beyond. As if to make up for how slowly my feet had moved before, I overshot my usual place in line. Instead of ending up at the end of the row, next to April, I came to a halt between my two sisters. April was to my left and Celeste to my right. We were out of order for the first and only time in our lives.

I faltered, appalled. For I was more than simply out of place, I was also directly in front of Monsieur LeGrand.

About the Author

CAMERON DOKEY is the author of nearly thirty young adult novels. Her most recent titles in the Once upon a Time series include *Wild Orchid, Belle, Sunlight and Shadow,* and *Before Midnight*. Her other Simon & Schuster endeavors include a book in the Simon Pulse Romantic Comedies line, *How NOT to Spend Your Senior Year*. Cameron lives in Seattle, Washington.

I look out the window,
and although it's dark,
the moon
illuminates the scene
as if a faraway
floodlight
is hung
from the sky.

So much whiteness.
Everywhere.

Come back,
angel.

Let us fly
away
from
here.

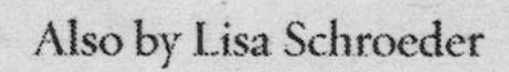
Also by Lisa Schroeder

From Simon Pulse | Published by Simon & Schuster